Praise for Aurora Stewart de Peña
and JULIUS JULIUS

"Aurora Stewart de Peña is pillar of the D.I.Y. indie performance art community, inspiring and mobilizing with her incisive and audacious projects."

—Sook-Yin Lee, director of *Paying for It*

"*Julius Julius* is the kind of satire I love, full of gentle wisdom and refusing to laugh at our expense. With imagination and tenderness, Stewart de Peña finds poetry in a pecuniary world of brand narratives and consumer manipulation, and asks us to forgive ourselves for buying in. This is a strange and beautiful book that wears big questions lightly."

—Martha Schabas, author of *My Face in the Light*

"A finely decorated glimpse into an advertising agency somehow floating outside of time. Stewart de Peña builds a dense, soft carpeted world of corridors that only an insider could give us, where the ad copy is so perspicuous it's educational. Despite its shadows (or because of them?), I would like to work at Julius Julius."

—Donovan Woods, *singer-songwriter*

"The rambling, mythic Agency reminded me at times of the enormous bathhouse from Hayao Miyazaki's *Spirited Away*, or the infinite labyrinth of Susanna Clarke's *Piranesi*, but ultimately could only be the creation of the singular imaginative force that is Aurora Stewart de Peña. A delight."

—Jordan Tannahill, author of *The Listeners*

"*Julius Julius* takes place at an advertising agency with a richly imagined, 2000-year history, housed in a labyrinthine building full of hidden wonders and lost souls. The novel is like that building: both unnerving and delightful, and made up of exquisite details. Aurora Stewart de Peña's debut is surreal in the way of a lucid dream, where anything could happen but everything makes sense. Throughout it all, the reader is warmly accompanied by Stewart de Peña's clear, congenial voice: *Julius Julius* is unsetting, sometimes terrifying, but shot through with humor and joy.

An award-winning playwright and advertising strategist, Stewart de Peña's one-of-a-kind sensibility, and devotion to craftsmanship, shines in everything she touches. She understands the art of creating ads, and the often amoral world of advertising—subjects that become captivating with her storytelling. Her understated absurdism recalls Flann O'Brien and Sarah Moss, while her imaginative rigor brings to mind Catherine Lacey, with Nicholson Baker's eye for small details that illuminate everything—she can derive a human epic from a tuna can.

Stewart de Peña is endlessly attentive to secret histories: the human drama that goes into creating a brand, or the human cost of erecting the buildings where our daily lives take place. A wholly original work of magic realism, *Julius Julius* immerses us in a strange and wonderful reality, while tuning our perception of the reality we know. *Julius Julius* is one of those rare novels that enlarges your attention in subtle, but indelible ways: the world seems bigger since I read it."

—Alexandra Molotkow, journalist

Aurora Stewart de Peña

JULIUS

JULIUS

A Novel

Copyright © 2025 by Aurora Stewart de Peña

First edition published 2025

All rights reserved. No part of this book may be reproduced, scanned, transmitted, or distributed in any form or by any electronic or mechanical means, including information storage and retrieval systems, without permission in writing from the publisher, except by a reviewer, who may quote brief passages in a review. No part of this book may be used or reproduced in any manner for the purpose of training artificial intelligence technologies or systems.

Strange Light is a registered trademark of
Penguin Random House Canada Limited.

The authorized representative in the EU for product safety and compliance is Penguin Random House Ireland, Morrison Chambers, 32 Nassau Street, Dublin D02 YH68, Ireland, https://eu-contact.penguin.ie

Library and Archives Canada Cataloguing in Publication Data
is available upon request.

ISBN: 978-0-7710-1514-4
ebook ISBN: 978-0-7710-1515-1

This is a work of fiction. Names, characters, places, and incidents either are the product of the author's imagination or are used fictitiously. Any resemblance to actual persons, living or dead, events, or locales is entirely coincidental.

Cover design: Matthew Flute
Cover art: (dachshund) CSA Images, (border) PATSTOCK / Getty Images
Typeset in Minion by Sean Tai
Printed in the United States of America

Published by Strange Light,
An imprint of Penguin Random House Canada,
320 Front Street West, Suite 1400
Toronto, Ontario, M5V 3B6, Canada
penguinrandomhouse.ca

1st Printing

For Scott

I *The Senior Brand Anthropologist*

II *The Creative Director*

III *The Future Leader (Intern)*

I *The Senior Brand Anthropologist*

II

I work at a very ancient ad agency. Situated beside the mall, it's in a big rambling building that takes up the entire block. From the outside, you can't even tell it's an ad agency. The sign is just a tiny plaque, and time has worn the letters away.

I chose a career in advertising because brands build our culture, and I wanted to feel important to culture.

I never thought I'd have this career, or any career at all. My plan after leaving home at fifteen was to live in a dirty apartment, look beautiful, and do a lot of drugs. I planned to go to parties, live to twenty-five, then die mysteriously, devastating the many people in love with me. I achieved the drugs, and sometimes people would compare me to Christina Ricci, but I hated the idea of anyone remembering me naked, so no one got the opportunity to fall in love. And obviously, I didn't die at twenty-five.

I've always loved ads. They're a parallel universe. People in advertising joke about having no souls, but finding success in this industry means believing that pure happiness is real. The most effective ads show us how optimism is rational. They imbue a product with it, and they're able to make that product a solution to people's sadness. And just before the moment of purchase, it is.

That little feeling before buying something is proof of an advertising person's soul.

I define "culture" as a set of shared feelings and ideas brought to life through expression. Those expressions influence us and impact the way we behave. Plays, books, movies, music, art, TV, essays, and photographs are the expressions people think of when they think of "culture." But you'll engage meaningfully with more ads during your life than any of those other things. And you have to seek out a movie or a play. And *then* you only spend a few hours with it. Ads come to you, wherever you are. And now, they reflect your deepest fears and unspoken desires.

Ads, whether we want to admit it to ourselves or not, are our real culture.

I can understand how that might sound like a capitalist nightmare, but it's actually okay. Ads can be beautiful. Or funny, or moving, or controversial. They reflect who we are. I think it's okay to sell something as long as you're giving something in return. Like a laugh, or a feeling.

When I'm within a hundred metres of the agency, I get a headache. It happened the first time I ever came here, for my interview. It's gotten worse throughout my employment. When I get on the streetcar to head to work, I pop a couple painkillers. I have a prescription for Goodheadrin.

My boss thinks the headaches are a reaction to the ultrasonic mouse repellers. They use the ones that plug into the walls and emit a high-pitched scream heard only by rodents. There are probably a thousand plugged in at our agency. We're not infested; it's a preventative measure. The building is so old, it's a mouse's paradise. So many crannies and nooks and centuries of dropped cheese.

My boss is obsessed with trying to get them removed, even though I'm the only one who gets headaches. I'm not entirely convinced they're the problem. A headache can't always be traced back to something real, like the noise from the repellers. I'm glad he has something to focus on, though. He's happiest when he's trying to make big operational changes.

Obviously, the headaches are my body trying to tell me something, but right now I cannot afford to listen. My career is on an upswing.

Every year, *Advertising Magazine* publishes a list of the most exceptional people in the industry, based on how many awards they've won. It's a page of headshots accompanied by labels like "The Rule-Breaker" or "The Risk-Taker." A very flattering write-up about the person's work accompanies each headshot. To get included on the list is a huge honour.

This year, they included me because of a digital banner campaign I worked on for a children's charity. They called me "The Thoughtful Maverick." A lot of people posted my write-up and congratulated me online, including an art director who I know hates me. His post meant a lot.

A local billionaire runs the children's charity. She inherited her money, so she can devote her time to raising awareness about the idea of adoption. Her charity is called Adoption Now!. Her father was a client at my old agency; he was the CEO of a grocery store chain. Our agency essentially did the campaign as a favour to her father, which worked out great for me.

My old boss gave me the project because of some previous work I'd done rebranding a line of frozen lasagnas. Instead of making the value proposition about convenience, I made it about the feeling of getting taken care of that comes from having prepared food at the ready. After my rebrand, all frozen lasagnas, not just the line I'd worked on, saw a bump in sales.

I'd never gotten to work on a charity before. It's a big deal at ad agencies, because you can make moving work that gets a lot of attention.

My campaign insight: thousands of foster kids live in the city, and no one seems interested in adopting them. But waiting lists to adopt pets are years-long. Research we conducted showed that people care more about sad dogs than they do about sad human children. But what if we could get them to think about children in need while already in the adopting mood? The creative seemed really simple: all we did was run a series of banner ads on pet adoption websites featuring the name and profile of a kid in the foster care system. The campaign was met with extreme success. We conducted a survey whose results showed an 11% increase in intention to adopt a child.

Making *Advertising Magazine*'s list meant I had my pick of agencies, which I'd never had before.

There are three reasons I decided to come work here:

- The place's incredible history. It's the oldest continuously operating ad agency in the world. I thought I'd inherit a legacy of ideas.
- My boss. I'd worked for him at another agency, and I learned so much from him. I felt sad when he left because this agency seemed unattainable to me and I thought I'd never see him again. Until I made the list. Of course, he's made the list many times ("The Wild Child"). He's a very beautiful person and famous in our industry. He's tall and wears a leather jacket and 22K-gold dog tags around his neck. He can work anywhere he wants. He's able to identify major cultural shifts just by observing what people wear to riots. He has perfect hair, and nobody has ever seen him touch it.
- Change is good. Change is important. She not busy being born is busy dying.

This agency can trace its roots back to Pompeii, around the year AD 79. It was named after our founder, a man named Julius Julius, who came up with the idea to drive lusty men to a specific chain of brothels by carving erect penises into the cobblestones of the surrounding area. They functioned as arrows, pointing men in the direction of pleasure.

His penises looked cartoony but still sexual enough to get his point across. The design's lighthearted concept drove business for the brothel. Many historians refer to these penises as the very first ads.

Julius Julius's renown began to spread, and soon he found himself carving sheaves of wheat for bakeries, proud horses for farriers, and heads full of flowing hair for hair oil merchants. As requests for his services grew, he took on two apprentices to help him meet the growing demand.

Of course, identifying "the first ad" is an impossible task, because ads look different in different cultures and economies, so an ad is pretty much anything that gets people to spend money on your business.

Also, people advertise intuitively. An ad might look like someone's good opinion of your services (influencer marketing), or choosing to place the sign for your business a little further down the road so that people see it as they walk by (out of home).

Textbooks love Julius Julius's penises because they can tie them to this agency, which makes a complete story, but also just because they're lazy enough to assume that ancient Rome serves as the genesis for everything. Merchants from Mesopotamia and the kingdom of Aksum probably hired people to carve out stones, too.

Julius Julius's agency is now a global entity with shops in 120 countries.

Julius Julius's original shop still operates today. It managed to survive the eruption of Mount Vesuvius in AD 79, the lava stopping mere feet away from the doorstep. Julius Julius himself survived, too. When the volcano exploded, most people fled for the shore, but of course the fast-flowing lava was hot enough to boil seawater, and the shifting of the ocean floor created a tsunami. But Julius Julius, an independent thinker, mounted his horse and galloped to the mountains, taking only his carving tools and a sketch of one of his original penises. He moved his main operations to Rome but kept the Pompeii location as a memorial to what was lost, eventually reopening it as a satellite.

Our shop obviously isn't the first—that would be the one in Pompeii—but it is considered a flagship. Our building is a historical landmark in the city. It's one of the few remaining that's still allowed to take up an entire city block for a single purpose. There used to be lots—boutique gyms, luxury stores— but a bylaw was passed decreeing that all buildings larger than 320,000 square feet had to have some space dedicated to affordable housing or community services. They made an exception for our ad agency because it is such a big part of the city's history.

I felt so excited to work here. The agency is responsible for many integral aspects of our culture. For instance:

- We trademarked the sound a can of Coca-Cola makes when you open it. The audio cue signals to consumers that something refreshing is coming. That's called sonic branding. Other soft drinks make a sound, but due to our trademark, theirs have to sound different.
- We normalized the idea of non-red lipstick in the 1930s, when, after a decade of aggressive, jazz-handing flappers in red, women who sought to evoke a softer version of femininity needed more options. Lipstick comes in many colours now, but a client of ours called Pif Paf Puf (bankrupt 1962) created the first non-red shade, called Petal Flush.
- A lot of people also credit our agency with establishing the shame that comes from not washing your hands after going to the bathroom. We ran a public service campaign called *Wash Up, Lasses!* targeted to volunteer nurses during the Crimean War. Knowledge about bacteria was not common, so to clean their hands, people would typically rub them on a crisp piece of linen and think they were fine. Our campaign featured images of sloppy, bare-breasted women dressed in stained linen teeming with visible bacteria accompanied by the copy "An unwashed lass spreads pestilence, her stink arouses the worst impulses in even the gentlest men." It hasn't aged well, but it worked. It was a strategy for a more sexually alarmist time.

In a couple weeks, I'll have worked at Julius Julius for six months. And I'm disappointed to report that all the incredible history hasn't translated into anything meaningful today. The agency has no vision, no North Star. I don't know what we stand for. The building is outdated, rambling, and uncomfortable. The fluorescent lights buzz and flicker, and the kitchen drawers are full of loose plastic forks. The partners are all men. There are six, and they're exactly the same person. They're from medium-good families, they hold centre-right politics, and they're tall. One of them occasionally wears suspenders, and because of this detail, the others call him Mr. Style. The muscles around the partners' mouths are tense, but because they want their colleagues to perceive them as good, fun guys, they'll flash an intentional toothy smile when they pass you in the hall. But when they're alone together, they cross their arms and their mouths get tense again. Sometimes I'll look into a boardroom and see them tense like that, and it empties my whole body of feeling.

My boss told me the agency wants to change. It is easy for men like the partners to tell someone like my boss that they want to change, because my boss, with his glass-walled house and art photography book collection, would look at the partners and think, *Obviously.* He'd take them at their word, because who wouldn't want to be more like him? He told me he was part of the agency's change. He would usher in a new era, and the people he hired, including me, would do it with him. I think he genuinely believes it's going to happen, but I don't. The partners have no interest in progress, or inclusivity, or anything. They just want people to like them, and right now, people like progressive and inclusive.

Good advertising changes the way we think. But great advertising changes the way we see the world. Great advertising reflects culture, amplifying ideas that move us all forward.

Any idiot can make a poster that tells you to wash your hands. Someone a little bit smarter will make a poster that shows you how, but if you've got other things on your mind, like serving as a nurse in the Crimean War, why would you take time away from treating soldiers screaming in pain to lather up?

A great advertiser will change the way you think about your hands. They'll make you understand that your hands are teeming with lethal bacteria. That your hands, the very things you use to heal, could inadvertently be responsible for the agony and death of hundreds of men. Men with families. Men with futures. Now, a nurse in the Crimean War perceives her hands differently.

Changing people's perceptions is a legacy I could feel proud about. I help people see the world in a way that benefits society. And while this agency isn't what I expected, it is the tool that I have to create my legacy, so I'm going to do my best with what I have.

We're pitching the Lumber Board. It's a government account. It's actually the one thing I'm excited about. It's not "sexy" like an athletic-apparel or automotive brand. In fact, the Lumber Board is barely a brand at all. But that's the exciting part! It's an opportunity to take a natural resource people have a very regular, functional relationship with and *elevate it into a brand*! People interact with lumber all day and night. They don't think about it, but they're intimate with lumber. Beds, tables, pencils: these things are lumber, and we use them every day. They might know what type of lumber it is if it's a luxury good, a solid pine pencil for instance, but usually that knowledge is eclipsed by their functional relationship to the lumber object. Chances are strong that the Lumber Board brand already exists in people's minds. If we win this pitch, my work will be to articulate it in a concise and relevant way.

Our agency interiors are famous worldwide. The lobby is decorated in white plastic and orange vinyl upholstery, but old and cracked. They initially did it during the Space Age. They had a plan to restore the plastic to like-new condition, but a historical design expert talked them out of it. As it turns out, aged plastic looks beautiful. Something created to represent the future, and here it is, getting old. There's poetry in that. It was featured in the online article "12 Iconic Ad Agency Lobbies" at number 12, which means it was the most iconic.

When you get further into the building, parts of the agency are wood and plaster, parts have concrete floors with graffiti murals on the walls, and there's one part that's a cave. The cave is the oldest room in the building, and a naturally occurring part of the ad agency. It's where the archives are. I try not to go down to the cave, because that's the area my stalker haunts, but sometimes I have no choice.

Yes, I have a stalker at work. He's a ghost. We have a lot of ghosts haunting our agency; the place is full of them. It's something everybody acknowledges, particularly when working late at night. Some are subtle; you'll feel like you're being watched and then the yogurt you had begun eating will disappear. Some are more obvious, like the transparent woman in a pencil skirt who wanders the halls distributing memos and crying.

Not everybody sees them, but we all feel them. That's what happens when you occupy a space the same way for a long time: you get ghosts.

It seems like a lot of them don't know they're dead and just keep doing their jobs. I think that's what happened to my stalker.

I used to love the cave and the archives. I would find reasons to go down to do research. The archivist who runs it is the most wonderful person here. She's a direct descendent of Julius Julius. She's very old (102!) and wears beautiful makeup. She was born in Rome, and she's always dripping in delicate gold jewelry. There are generations of rejuvenating skin-care treatments mapped out on her face. Her knuckles are swollen; they look like they hurt. She types one finger at a time. She sits at a sage-green desk from the 1950s between the hours of one and five in the afternoon, Monday to Friday. It's a perfect job, I think.

Everything we've ever made, dating back to ancient Rome, is in the archives. Almost twenty miles of filing cabinets and billboards. It runs under the city like the catacombs in Paris, and it's almost as big. The cave is a real cave; it's cool and dark, and there are stalagmites and stalactites. It smells old, like wet stone, and it's full of plastic plants. At first, I thought fake plants seemed like an odd choice, but they keep it from feeling too alien.

My stalker works in the Underground Annex. It's the part of the cave next to the archives. It's a tiny room lit by electric wall sconces that look like candles. The interior designers salvaged the sconces from a chain of steakhouses called Beefsteak Charlie's. They used to have locations all over the prairies when they were our client, but they went bankrupt in 1987.

The Underground Annex is where HR moves people they hope will quit. They make them spend all their time in a dark, musty, inconvenient place. It takes at least twenty-five minutes to get to the cave via our very old elevator and a tunnel car. There's also a very large, deep subterranean pond full of translucent shrimp in the middle of the room, so your clothes are always a bit damp. Even worse, there's a colony of white millipedes who live on the walls of the cave, and they make an audible scuttling sound when they move. The administrative assistants won't call an exterminator because, apparently, they're an endangered species.

If someone's desk is moved to the Underground Annex, everybody knows they've done something wrong but that they're not important enough for the agency to fire and pay severance to. Almost nobody who gets moved down there gets moved back up. Once, an account executive who had sex with a client got moved down, then she had sex with one of the partners, married him, and got moved back up again. I remember her, because she used to wear sunglasses on top of her head as her regular hairstyle, even when it rained. In retrospect, she was good at her job. She could have worked anywhere.

The first time I saw my stalker, I was making an appointment to see *Wash Up, Lasses!* There's a three-month wait, because it's fragile and they try to limit exposure. They do make reproductions available—mimeographs. I took one; I think it might serve as a useful reference for the Lumber Board pitch.

Wash Up, Lasses! is worth the wait. It's a historic piece of work, like the advertising version of the *Mona Lisa*. I've never had access to anything like it. Hopefully I don't get murdered before my appointment day arrives.

As the archivist began entering my information for the appointment, I felt hot breath on the back of my neck. When I turned around, I saw my stalker's back walking through the wall of the cave. He wore a voluminous button-up shirt tucked into pleated khaki pants.

There are a lot of creeps down here, the archivist said. *The bats are the least of it.* I told her I found bats cute. She shook her head in the way people do when they fundamentally disagree with you but understand there's no point in arguing. I told her it was a myth that they get tangled in your hair. *No, it's not*, she said, laughing a little. She wore a St. Francis of Assisi medal, and it caught the light.

When I first met the archivist, I caught myself thinking she was too old to work. But what do I know? The average age of an ad agency employee is thirty-one years old. It felt nice to see wrinkles. We smoke together. She gives me dating advice. In return, I pretend I'm someone who goes on dates.

One of my favourite pieces of her advice: to check if someone is attracted to me, drop something small, like a pencil or a glove, and see if they pick it up. If they do, it means they're interested and paying attention to my movements. That's enough to begin flirting.

I'm not undatable, by the way. I'm not a supermodel or anything. I'm probably a 5.5 or a 6. I'd feel fine if I could find anyone
worth liking. But the only place I go where there are men is
work. And every man at work is so monumentally boring that
I'm better off going home, masturbating, and thinking about
nothing.

Legend has it that when my stalker was alive, he worked as an account guy. That's not surprising, given that I've only ever met two good account guys. The rest are terrible. Account guys anchor every interaction they have in their desire to keep things medium. Their outfits always look neat, and they style their hair aggressively. Usually, they'll have an exaggerated interest in something masculine, like barbecue sauce. They don't want you to become interested; they just want you to perceive them as a person with interests.

Never tell an account guy about a dream you had, because he'll swear he can't remember his dreams. I hate that. Everyone has woken up from at least one dream that destroyed them. But these account guys are so committed to maintaining blandness that they can't even admit they've got a subconscious.

Women who work in accounts are a completely different story. Ad agencies would fall apart without Account women.

As soon as I'm done work, I'm exhausted. It's because of the combination of overhead lighting, overhearing conversations, and spending time around others breathing and suppressing their feelings. It drains me. There's nothing left by the time I get home. My body just wants to fall asleep. But if I let that happen, I won't ever do anything. So I set a series of alarms and use them to time out non-advertising activities.

I read for twenty minutes; I run for forty minutes; I spend twenty minutes in the shower, thirty minutes journalling; and I let myself watch TV or a movie for two hours to wind down. I set that alarm because if I don't, I will fall asleep on the couch.

There are two reasons I don't let myself fall asleep on the couch:

- I'll get a stiff neck.
- Night terrors. I get them every time I pass out on the couch watching TV. I wake up in the middle of the night and I can't move; it's as though I'm paralyzed. In the corner of the living room, a dark figure appears—a person in the shadows. As he moves toward the couch, I can feel there's something off about the situation. He's blurry, like an out-of-focus photo. I can't quite see his face, or the details of his clothes, and only know he's a man. He holds a pillow from my bedroom, gripping it tightly, and when he does his knuckles peak sharply. Suffocating me is his goal. I attempt to get up, but can't, and then at the last moment, when he's standing over me, he fades out like an image on a TV that got turned off because I accidentally rolled on the remote. Then I'm alone again, in the dark living room, on the couch. It can take my body minutes to figure out how to move again. I never trust myself to fall back asleep after. I stay up until sunrise. These terrors don't ever happen when I sleep in my bedroom.

This new role came with a pretty substantial pay raise. I'm using it to decorate my apartment. It's amazing how many things you realize you don't have as soon as you get the money to buy them. My dream is to create an apartment that reflects my taste exactly. I've gone through three laundry hampers in the past year because I can't find one that reflects my aesthetic. Once I saw a woven-grass, pineapple-shaped hamper online I loved. That was last year and it was a little over my price range at the time so, sadly, I didn't buy it. I regret that. If you see something that's perfect for you, you have to just go for it.

I would never try to define my aesthetic. I would never say *I like a rustic style* or *I like a minimalist style.* The second you try to define it, you're using somebody else's style to describe yours. That puts you in danger of losing sight of what it is you truly like.

I'm meticulous about getting rid of things. Clutter builds up fast. I go through all my things once every two weeks. In each room, I've got a pile of items designated for donation. It's made of things:

- That no longer reflect my taste
- That are broken
- That are infused with bad psychic energy, like if I used them a lot when depressed

There's a lot in that last category. Technically nothing wrong with them, but they're steeped in awful feelings. I have sticky energy. I almost feel bad about getting rid of them, because then I'm passing that energy on to another person. But maybe those people have enough good energy to counteract mine. Or maybe it's like cilantro: for me, it feels toxic, but for them, it's just a dress.

I barely had to interview for this job. That should have been a red flag. Because I'd already worked with my boss at my previous agency, it's not like he had to check references. I did meet one person, a woman who had the title Senior Talent Acquisition Officer. She's in her early fifties and has pale pink hair. She asked me if I like to drink wine on Wednesdays and said it with a wink, because it was a Wednesday. She told me the place was like a family, the partners were like her brothers. She told me the agency has a philosophy: *paradigm shifts happen when everyone shifts the paradigm together*. I still don't know what I'm supposed to do with that.

I'd dressed up and put together a portfolio, an actual physical portfolio with a leather cover. But I didn't even get the chance to open it. She didn't want to see anything because she'd heard such great things about me. Instead, she told me about herself. I learned that she had been a ceramicist but became a talent acquisition officer because she needed to earn a salary. She told me she still did ceramics on the side and occasionally sold them on Agency Craft Market Day.

I remember noticing that the carpets in the lobby had stains all over them. That's unusual in places designed to welcome status-conscious clients.

I have the landing page for the pineapple hamper open in my tabs, still.

It's called the Ananas Fair Trade Hamper, and the makers wove it close to the island of Guadeloupe, where pineapples grow. Pineapples swept through Europe as a design theme in the seventeenth century after explorers brought them back from Guadeloupe. Everyone thought they were the best fruit they'd ever tasted. I can believe it. Imagine tasting pineapple for the first time, no context? You would lose your mind. The write-up for the Ananas hamper says it's woven using traditional techniques and straw made from palm, which is one of nature's strongest weaving materials. If I'd bought the hamper like I originally wanted to, 10% of the funds from the purchase would have gone to support school lunch programs for the children of local weavers.

My title is Senior Brand Anthropologist.

My boss and I thought for a long time about my title. We wanted it to be an accurate but unique reflection of my skill set and daily activities. I immerse myself in our target audience, I study the way they act and behave, I try to figure out why they do the things they do so I can guide the brands I work on to speak to them more effectively. I *do* think of myself as an anthropologist, studying and interpreting human behaviour. It's not just a cute title.

One thing I actually love about Julius Julius is the dogs. The building is a habitat for a medium-sized pack of blonde sausage dogs. They've lived here for generations, and they're quite friendly and cute. They have silky hair, and their tails wag slower than average. The original pair of dogs belonged to a creative director who worked here decades ago. For generations, people have remembered him as just the nicest guy. That's reflected in his dogs, or, rather, his dogs' descendants. He and the original dogs have been dead for some time now. There's a portrait of him in the King Koffee boardroom, painted in the style of the Dutch masters. The dogs are in his lap, and they have big dog smiles on their faces.

Technically, the responsibility of feeding and walking the dogs falls on the executive assistants, but everybody pitches in because they're so loved.

The executive assistants are a troop of beautiful, thin young women. Every one of them. That's not unique to our agency; it's consistent across the industry. When we think of all the advancements women have made, it's shocking to me that the senior men can't imagine anyone other than a tight-butted girl scheduling their appointments. I'm not saying they're not good at their jobs, but give a fat dad a chance.

Right now, I work on:

- Fizzy-Bub
- The NHSTT (National High-Speed Transit Train)
- Agatha Brand Menstrual Cups
- The Preventing Cancer Association

Technically a great portfolio, but existentially boring. I don't like working on any of it. That's why I really want to win the Lumber Board account. Right now, all I want to do is shop. I can do the majority of my work in two hours, and then I spend the rest of the day looking at hampers and other interior design objects online. I love that little hit of dopamine that comes from clicking "checkout"—the only dopamine I can access regularly.

He'd never admit it, but my boss only put me on Agatha because I'm a woman. I guess it's better than having someone who doesn't use cups on the account, but it's just so predictable. He said that after many years of functional advertising (leak-proof, moves with you, etc.), the brand needed to differentiate itself from other feminine hygiene products by building a stronger emotional connection to the people who use it. I get all the emotional connection brands. Another guy here gets cellphones and chocolate bar brands that get to make jokes. I guess I should consider it a compliment. My boss told me I was an empath. I said, *That must be why I want to kill myself.* He didn't think it was funny. He asked me if I was okay. I said, *Oh, I'd never joke about wanting to kill myself if it were actually true.*

Every year, our ad agency hosts a big holiday party for our clients. We're told it's something they look forward to. There's an open bar, a theme, and piles of food. This year, the theme was Leather 'n' Studs. So we all dressed up like punks, bikers, and daddies. The agency bought mountains of burgers and fries and a bar full of SKYY Vodka. One of my colleagues got so drunk she fell asleep on a table with a half-eaten Twinkie in her mouth. The party raged around her. But she passed out cold, and the vanilla filling mixed with her drool to create a foam that dribbled down her chin. I wanted to put her in a cab and take her home. But the partners thought she was fantastic: *She's contributing to the vibe.*

They wanted it to feel like a real party. Apparently, the clients loved it; they all took pictures.

That night, there was a power outage for a full fifteen minutes. It was the whole block, so it was the whole building. When the lights went out, people began screaming. Not a scared scream, but like a roller-coaster scream. I tried joining in, but I had trouble getting my voice to work.

Also that night, I went back to my work area to switch out my shoes and found five blonde sausage dogs huddled together under my desk. They wanted to escape the party, I guess. They looked at me with their big sausage dog eyes, and the littlest one tilted her head up and let out a tiny howl. I crawled under the desk with them and sat for a bit. The little howler crawled into my lap and fell asleep. Her name is Biscotti. All the sausage dogs have bone-shaped name tags engraved with their Roman names.

A Pompeiian baker, Sabina Saturnina, invented biscotti around AD 67 for Roman soldiers to take on their expeditions. She also invented a special twice-baked process. The first baking cooked the dough, and the second baking preserved the cookies so they stayed good for a long time. Pliny the Elder used to say that Sabina Saturnina's biscotti would remain edible for generations. Julius Julius created a billboard for Sabina Saturnina's bakery and installed it on the road out of town. The idea was to catch the legions before they set out. It was a carved plaque reading "Edible for Generations" next to a portrait of Pliny the Elder.

Biscotti the dog visits with me. I keep treats for her. She falls asleep under my desk with her fuzzy little chin on my toes. *They're friendly to everybody, but they don't love everybody*, the archivist told me. I feel chosen. I do love Biscotti.

Brands build culture in two ways, intentionally and unintentionally.

Brand-building the unintentional way means they buy ad space everywhere, and they sponsor everything. Their only goal is to make people think of them at every turn. If you see enough pictures of a frosty, refreshing Coke, you will eventually want one. These brands become our cultural wallpaper and form our collective consciousness.

When brands build culture intentionally, they approach ad placements and sponsorships with a lot of care, precision, and intention. They'll develop relationships with artists and athletes; they'll sponsor music scenes and sports competitions. These brands can make big things possible in culture. For instance, Airwalk sponsored the fifth ever Lollapalooza. Because of this sponsorship, the festival was able to have a skate ramp. Culture-building brands fuse themselves to the ideas and feelings that feed us. If you picture the Ramones, they're wearing Converse. If you picture LeBron James, he's wearing Nikes.

Given the choice, I prefer to work on brands that take the intentional approach, understand their impact, and generally have good intentions. There's a big difference in the personality of the clients, too. They want to be part of a bigger story and to contribute to the cultural conversation.

The clients who take the unintentional approach are unintentional about everything else, too. They just want to make money so they can buy their glitzy little items. They fill their lives with expensive places and objects, never even stopping to ask themselves whether or not they like them.

Today was the day of the Lumber Board pitch. I wore a black ribbed turtleneck, a black pleated maxi skirt, and black ankle boots. My colleague wore a black jumpsuit with a black blazer and black stilettos. Her outfit worked better for the pitch. I need to remember for next time: wearing pants makes a better first impression, because then you won't come across as fussy. When clients see me, I want them to see a smart, cohesive package, not an outfit.

I think the pitch went really well. At least I hope it did. I loved working on it. I don't often get to think about something that grows from the earth. To open the pitch presentation, we put together a video of forests, tables, trees, chairs, branches, and counters, all things made of wood. It was quite moving. It surprised me how much thinking about lumber made me feel.

Developing the central pillars of the presentation felt meditative, and I was inspired to write them in more poetic language than usual.

Pillar #1: Lumber has been our ally since the beginning of time: we walk among trees, their shade has always protected us.

Pillar #2: We turn to lumber for all our most basic activities: we eat at wooden tables, we sleep on wooden bed frames.

Pillar #3: The lumber brand is already inside us; our work is only to articulate it.

It played well in the room. The clients leaned forward and asked great questions. At the end, each member of our team added an anecdote about how lumber had affected them personally. Mine was that when I am feeling hopeless and alone, lying on my hardwood floor is a steadfast source of comfort. It wasn't as much of a downer as you might think. Clients actually like to know their agency team emotionally invests in their brand.

The only problem with the pitch was that my stalker was there. When I'd get up to speak, I'd see him seated with clients, or leaning in the corner of the room alongside the office administrators. Always just out of the corner of my eye. It distracted me. I hope the clients didn't notice. He made the room really cold, though. Probably so my nipples would get hard. He's such an asshole.

I haven't told anyone about my stalker except the archivist. I hate talking about sexual harassment stuff. It happens to everybody and it happens so frequently and I'm not special because it's happening to me. When I told her, she said, *Just because it happens to everyone does not mean it should.*

She told me my stalker had worked in the cave for a period of time when he was alive and, during that time, had left drawings of his penis on the archivist's desk accompanied by notes that went, like, "Want to see the real deal? Swing by my desk sometime." *He is just absolutely stupid,* she said.

She told me that she'd once gotten sexually harassed, but she didn't go into detail. *That story is for a longer cigarette than the one I've got lit,* she said. *Another time.*

The archivist gave me a copy of his file. It's this big thick stained manila file folder packed with crackling, whispery old paper.

Keep it, she said. *Information is power.*

I took it home and read it in bed.

My stalker got fired for multiple incidents of sexual harassment. Seventy-nine separate complainants had come forward about him, each reporting hundreds of individual incidents, which means we can assume there had actually been thousands. I guess I'm not surprised.

He'd done all the usual stuff, like make sexually explicit comments and grab butts, but there were also a few reports of him breaking into co-workers' houses at night, stealing their pillows, and rubbing them on his naked body while he took a shower in their bathroom. They'd wake up to a steamy bathroom and wet pillow full of pubic hair.

As a ghost, he can't do much. He hovers around my cubicle, peeking his head over my partition. He leaves me things, weird items that look like work, a receipt or a tear sheet from an old print campaign. He'll also leave vaguely sexual objects: bottles of baby powder, tampons from the bathroom. And he steals my stuff. I'll put my laptop down and then it will be gone. When I trace it, it's usually in one of the older parts of the agency, the areas he'd have worked in when he was alive. And, of course, if I am in an important meeting or presenting anything, he's always in the group, fading in and out.

In the file, there are photos of him. Photos from holiday parties, photos from around the office. He styled his hair in an exaggerated pompadour. The notes describe how his clients loved him. He had charm, was efficient, and went the extra mile. I asked the archivist why so many flattering testimonials were included in a sexual harassment case file, and she told me it was because the partners at the time wanted to make sure they had a well-rounded perception of him before they made any decisions that could harm his career.

My stalker got fired forty-one years after the first wave of complaints had gone on file. In the first year that he worked at the agency, eight people had gone to HR about him, and six mentioned him as the primary reason reason for quitting in their exit interviews. He started as an intern when he was twenty-three, and he got fired when he was sixty-four and leading the Frosted Flakes account.

The partners shuffled him from account to account, department to department, until they moved him down to the cave. When he got inappropriate with the archivist, she reported it. Because she'd worked there for so long, they finally took it seriously.

The story goes that he got fired, then went home and died that night.

I didn't go to the funeral, the archivist told me. *Fuck him.*

But then he showed up to work the next morning like nothing had happened, except now he was a ghost. Of course, that put the agency in a difficult position because then they *really* couldn't get rid of him.

I left the file on my bedside table overnight. I think it affected my sleep. The smell of the musty old paper kept waking me up, and I dreamt about bats.

This morning, in the shower, I found a bar of soap that wasn't mine. I use a locally produced natural soap made from honey, almonds, and goat milk. This soap was Irish Spring. It sat on the edge of the bathtub, which is not where I keep my soap. I keep my soap in a wire hanger suspended from the nozzle. Whoever used the bar of Irish Spring had done so a few times. Pubic hairs had embedded themselves in the cake. How long had it sat there? A long time, maybe. I never look in that corner of the shower.

Of course, my immediate suspicion is that it's my stalker's ghost's soap, but I feel like I'm being paranoid. He's never come to my house before, I don't think. For my own mental health, I can't let myself jump to that conclusion. I did bring a guy home about two months ago, and I think he took a shower afterwards. It's possible that he travelled with his own soap and left it there. I really can't remember the last time I examined that corner of the shower. I'm going through a phase where I'm not cleaning as much. Maybe it's always been there. Maybe it was there when I moved in.

Irish Spring made one of my favourite TV commercials of all time. In it, a hopeless miner who spends his life in the dark receives a bar of Irish Spring from a beautiful woman with wavy red hair. Then he's magically whisked away to a sunny waterfall in the rolling green hills of Ireland, where he lathers up joyfully, tilting his face up to the sky. He feels the sun on his skin for the first time in decades. That commercial is so simple and so sensory: the grit of the mine; the fresh, clean waterfall; the warmth of the sun. It's become a cultural artifact. *Saturday Night Live* spoofed it. That's one of the metrics of cultural iconography.

I wonder if the people who made the Irish Spring ad were being intentionally culture-building. I don't know if they were. The ad is so singular in its message—the coal miner in the waterfall might really have been the most effective way to sell the soap. Soap ads in the past had focused on pragmatic messaging, like how perfectly the bar fit into your hand or what percentage of body odour smells it reduced. Making the same claims for Irish Spring would have just been shouting into the crowd, and that's not effective communication.

Instead, the team on Irish Spring were able to illustrate the feeling of the soap—really, the feeling of showering—and attribute it to their brand.

Comparing a shower to a waterfall isn't mind-blowingly original, but if your commercial means that people buying your soap imagine themselves in a waterfall when they're in their regular showers, you've given them a much more powerful feeling of clean than they'll ever get with a bar that fits their hand or reduces bad odours 10% more than the competition.

More importantly, you've given office workers and retail staff and waiters permission to imagine themselves as coal miners, beaten down and hopeless from hours labouring in the dark mines. And you have made yourself the water and the light.

Maybe intentions don't matter. After enough time, everything that's stayed around for long enough is part of culture. Coke, soap, sneakers, it's all about people's experiences with them over time, and it doesn't even matter what people at ad agencies do. I read once that people considered Charles Dickens trashy in his day, and the reason he wrote long books wasn't because he got inspired to tell a grand tale, but because he got paid by the word. Maybe Irish Spring is like Charles Dickens. They only wanted to sell soap but ended up making something beautiful by accident.

There's something optimistic about that. We're trying so hard to connect with each other that every expression of human creativity will do it, eventually.

Right now, my favourite room in the agency is the formal boardroom on the fifth floor. Each floor has a formal board-room dedicated to high-ranking clients. It's usually decked out in their products and branding. They designed this one for King Koffee coffee makers. They're still a client of ours, but we don't see the C-suite very often.

That happens, sometimes. A CEO will get old and refuse to work, and you basically have to wait for him to die and some-one else to get hired in order to get time with the guy at the top. In King Koffee's case, the CEO has remained housebound in Atlanta, Georgia, for almost ten years now. He's a stereo-typical old billionaire with a blanket over his knees and a very young wife. I've heard he used to be quite square-jawed and spectacular in his prime.

The fifth floor used to serve as the top floor, until they built three more floors above it. There was a glass ceiling that used to show off the sky, but now it shows off sixth-floor accounting. They wear a lot of sneakers up there. You can see the soles through the ceiling.

So the agency has basically abandoned the King Koffee board-room, but it's still so nice. All maple wood furniture, carpeting on the floors and walls, and a huge chandelier from the 1980s made of brown glass tubes. There are ten sterling silver King Koffee machines, and six of them still work. There's a big long glossy maple wood table. I crawl under there when I need to cry. Nobody ever comes in. Well, once somebody else came in, an intern who also needed to cry. I haven't seen her since, though. Bet she got fired.

One of the first things you must do when starting out at a new agency is figure out where to cry. If there is no abandoned boardroom, I recommend a back stairwell or the part of the garage where people keep their bikes, somewhere fairly low traffic. I would not recommend the washroom, which is high traffic. If people hear you, they might try to comfort you, and that feels even worse than crying.

The building is a maze, so you'd think there'd be a million places to cry, but it's well-lit and busy everywhere, even in unexpected places. I've gotten lost and found myself in departments I didn't know existed trying to find a place to cry. There's a department here that prints vintage versions of our clients' logos on t-shirts. There are sixty people who work in that department! It's very successful. You don't know you want a t-shirt with a 1976 Great Lakes Financial logo on it until you see it. There's a department that develops characters for TV and movies to personify brands. Sam from *iCarly* was 7 Up, for instance. She's youthful, bubbly, and a bit acidic. She never actually drank 7 Up on the show—she just embodied it—so after watching an episode, you crave a 7 Up, but you don't know why. That department is full of people staring critically at walls full of headshots bearing sticky notes that say things like "warm . . ." and "vibrant???????"

For context, most ad agencies are built all at once and have a cohesive design vision. My old ad agency was all marble with light wood and brass. The art on the walls was graffiti, but only in the agency colours, which were purple, yellow, hot pink, and sky blue. You never come across anything you don't expect, and it's certainly never disorganized. There are no unexpected corners. Walls are hard to find, and when you do find them, they're made of glass.

If a wall is glass, does that make it a window, technically? I just thought of that.

This agency was built over the course of a very, very, very long time. They added parts without any thought about the parts that came before or the parts that would come after. New partners are minted and they decide to take the agency in a completely different direction, burying the old directions to get decoded by whoever comes across them.

This morning, I discovered my stalker had pinned one of the mimeographs of *Wash Up, Lasses!* to the wall of my cubicle. The ink is that bleary purple, and it has that glue smell. I guess I don't know for sure that it's my stalker, but it seems like something he'd do. I asked my cubicle mates if any of them had seen who'd done it and one of them said, *I thought you did.* No one ever pays attention to anything.

I left it up. I don't want him to know it freaked me out. You can't let ghosts know they're scaring you: it just gives them more power.

I wonder if my stalker is trying to tell me I'm a pestilence-spreading slut who needs to wash up? Could that also be what the soap in my shower is about? Or is *Wash Up, Lasses!* the most pornographic image he can get his hands on and he's doing whatever he can to sexualize my desk area?

Last night, I woke up angry at 3 a.m., thinking about *Wash Up, Lasses!* Something had just occurred to me. It's a poster targeted toward women, presumably nurses, to remind them to wash their hands before dealing with wounded soldiers. But in my research, I found that Florence Nightingale, famous nurse Florence Nightingale, had introduced hygienic operations to the military hospital where these posters were hung. Before Florence Nightingale and her nurses, hospitals were disgusting. There are reports of soldiers with open infected wounds lying around in their own excrement in rooms with no windows and filthy walls and beds full of lice. So why are the lasses the target of the poster? The poster should be telling everyone *but* the lasses to wash up. The lasses are clean. The lasses invented clean. I think the assumption was that women fear that they're dirty no matter what, so they'll stay extra vigilant, and men will do whatever they can, including washing up, for the world to perceive them as better and cleaner than women.

Yesterday, I got a slew of notifications that unrecognized devices, obsolete technologies, had tried to log into my accounts. They included a Commodore 64, an ICON computer, and a pager—at least twenty old devices in total. I got locked out of my banking app because someone had tried to log in with the wrong password too many times.

I talked to our IT guy. He told me the IP addresses associated with the logins were all just different emojis and punctuation marks. He said, *I've never seen anything like this before.* There's no way to trace it back to anyone, so there's nothing he can do about it.

I've always found our IT guy very attractive. He has a wide-open face and makes undemanding eye contact. He's so handsome, I accidentally told him about my stalker ghost. He told me that when he's working late, the transparent woman who distributes memos and cries will come stand by his desk and just stare at him.

Be careful, he told me.

I am careful every single day of my life and have been ever since
I was born.

A brand is the sum total of every idea and experience a customer has about or with a product. Package design, service, architecture of store and offices, reviews people leave on the internet, everything. Advertisers say they "build brands," but really, people collectively imagine brands together. All advertisers can do is try to guide that imagining.

Often it works, but sometimes it doesn't. Anytime a brand has tried to turn into something completely new, or break away from people's previous experiences with it, it gets rejected. You can't lie in advertising. You can't even really self-aggrandize. People aren't stupid, unfortunately.

A brand, above all else, must be true.

People love to say they hate advertising. It makes them feel smart. But half the time, they don't even know they're being advertised to.

There are obvious instances of being advertised to: things like seeing commercials on TV or driving past a billboard on the highway. These are the kinds of ads people take pride in hating. The ones that interrupt. But today, a lot of advertising slides so seamlessly into our lives that we don't even notice it.

For instance, at my old agency, we once had an international bank as our client. A couple of years ago, they decided to create a program to give loans to small businesses. They had some research that told them they lost clients to credit unions because people wanted to feel a personal connection to their financial institution, so the bank decided to invest in local community.

Because we were responsible for guiding their brand, we were consulted about what that program could be. The bank's corporate mission was to Give Everyone in the World the Right to Thrive and Feel Secure. Their vision was a Financially Stable Global Community.

We looked at what the bank has meant to people historically (security, establishment) and what it wanted to mean in the future (equity). I should say now that though the bank hadn't traditionally stood for equity, now it wanted to. The bank had recently defined its three core brand values, and one of them was inclusivity.

Knowing this, we worked with the bank to develop a program to support small businesses run by *women.*

Women had not traditionally been given the right to thrive (by this bank or any bank); in fact, they are still the least financially stable people around the globe. We did consumer research that showed funding small businesses run by women would help people understand the bank as an inclusive entity (there's a reason one of the core values was inclusivity: 63% of consumers worldwide report valuing it), then we brought that research back to the bank and they basically had no choice but to agree that a program funding small businesses run by women would be great for their brand. The program was born.

Anyone interacting with it today would have no idea that FemStart was a brand-building exercise for the bank, but here we are.

I was very proud to be part of that project. Advertising can be a force for good.

Despite changing all my passwords on every single one of my accounts, I'm still getting two or three notifications of suspicious activities every day. This week, I've also begun getting emails. I think it's safe to assume they're from my stalker.

Sometimes they're just the rhinoceros emoji or the purple devil; sometimes they're blank. I was ignoring them, but today I got one that actually had text in it:

So you remember me??? I'm the dunce sloth who was too stupid to see the angel in front of him . . . .
. . . . .
. . . . .
. . . . .
. . . . .
. . . . .
. . . . .
. . . . . jogs your memory.
HAHAHAHAHAHAHA! I was watching and you did a good job today. You have charm, but you're completely unaware of it. That's what I like about you. Innocenti.

The next morning, I got another email.

Here's a picture of me, let's see if you recognize the face that knows you better than you know yourself and LOVES you even more . . . . . .

In the body of the email was a cropped picture of traffic lights, like one square of a captcha.

I went to IT again, but the guy who helped me before had been transferred to Luxembourg, and I had to talk to a new guy. The IP addresses that had sent the emails were the punctuation marks and emojis again. It was entirely too exhausting to get into the whole story about my stalker, so I just told him there'd been some attempted logins on my account and then this. He was less freaked out about it than the handsome guy. His theory involved an email malfunction.

I hadn't considered something like that. Like maybe there's a glitch and I'm getting emails meant for other people. Or maybe I'm getting emails from the past. Emails that got stuck in the server, deteriorating.

That seems like too big of a coincidence, but it's a comforting thought.

When I think about my stalker, I feel bad for him. I know I'm not supposed to. But in his file, it said he had never married and never had children, and that he only had one friend at work: a middle-aged senior copywriter who wore a frayed baseball cap with sunglasses perched on the brim. Despite his probable loneliness, my stalker came in early every morning and he stayed late every night.

Most people at ad agencies are always at work. That's why a lot of them get married to each other. Not my stalker, but a lot of people. A lot of them also get divorced because they never come home.

There are dozens of pictures of my stalker smiling at parties in his file, and I'll bet every single one of those parties took place at work. Those parties are also where most of his incidents took place. He'd get drunk, grab someone hard enough to bruise them, then tell them he was in love with them (holiday party); he'd slide next to someone in a booth, dead-eyed and inebriated, suck on their earlobe, and try to slide his hand between their thighs (drinks at the pub after a pitch); he'd announce his plans to marry a colleague to a table full of people, then beg that person to look at his dick, which he had already taken out (client dinner). The partners laughed it off the next day until they didn't.

He did harass people during the day and would whack butts and whistle as people walked by, but then, according to reports, he would blush furiously and refuse to speak if someone called him on it.

Some psychological complexities at work, there.

I imagine him lonely, working to the point of burnout, painfully shy, then drunk, desperate for connection and physical intimacy, then waking up the next day in a shame panic and doing his best to avoid the situation. He must have felt so insecure.

I told my boss.

It felt like the right thing to do, before I did it.

We had sat in the back seat of a cab, him on the way to a dinner I wasn't invited to. In the morning, I'd asked him if he had ten minutes to talk about something important. He said his day was jam-packed, but he'd find some time. I barely saw him all day, just caught glimpses of his long legs in tapered pants rushing around below our cubicle walls. At about five in the afternoon, he came over to my desk and said, *Oh, do you still want to chat?* I told him I did. That's how I ended up in the back of his cab. Before we left, I had three shots of tequila to calm my nerves and he said, *Whoa, slow down, that's the good stuff*, so I made myself an espresso to cancel out the liquor. We got in the car and I tried to make small talk about what had happened at the Lumber Board pitch before I decided to just get it over with.

I took a deep breath and told him that a ghost had begun stalking me, had maybe left soap in my apartment, and had definitely broken into my computer. Then the tequila hit me. My boss's face had the same tight expression the partners usually wore, one I hadn't seen on him before. He braced himself against the door of the car, gripping the handle. *I believe you*, he said. But I didn't believe him. That's what you're supposed to say. I noticed his pants were a dark silver colour, almost pewter. *I like your pants*, I said and then immediately regretted it. *What do you want to do about this?* he asked. I told him I didn't know, but I thought I should tell somebody what I was dealing with in case it affected my work. He agreed. I told him I should probably get a new phone.

If you wanted a new phone, you could have just asked, he said. I tried to laugh and so did he.

Not the cathartic experience I had hoped for.

I didn't go home after. I went back to the agency and up to the King Koffee boardroom, where I crawled under the table and cried. Biscotti the blonde sausage dog came and snuggled into my stomach. I matched my breathing to hers, and the two of us fell asleep curled together under my coat.

We woke up the next morning, before lunch. No one had come in at all, not even the cleaning staff. I took a wet wipe to my face, went downstairs, and started work. No one said anything. No one commented that I was late or that I was wearing the same clothes as yesterday. No one commented on the carpet marks on my face.

My boss did make sure IT got me a new phone. I found it on my desk with a bottle of the tequila I'd drunk too much of and a handwritten note that said *seems like ur going thru a rough time*.

It's the latest model, and the security features are supposedly next-level. I don't think security features will help me, but I don't want to seem ungrateful. I do like having a new phone. I wasn't supposed to get upgraded for another six months.

My headaches are getting worse. They start as soon as I wake up now. There are a few moments before I open my eyes when I think, *Oh, I don't have a headache yet*, but then the headache hears my thoughts and comes in strong.

Generally, the dogs won't go down to the cave. But recently someone found Biscotti down there after the entire building filled with her howling. The sound came up through the vents, bouncing off the walls of the elevator shaft, making the whole agency sad. They sent an executive assistant down to look and found her shivering, adrift on a piece of wood in the middle of the pond in the Underground Annex. She had water bugs in her fur and a dead shrimp clinging to her paw. It's obvious she didn't go down there by herself. How could she have? My boss asked me if I thought it had anything to do with my stalker, and I told him I thought it did, because Biscotti and I are friends. He nodded gravely, which is all he or anyone can do.

They took her to the vet, and we learned that she's pregnant, expecting puppies. She's made a home for herself under my desk again, nestled between a box of historical menstrual cup files and my presentation shoes. I bought her a little covered bed so she can disappear from the world when she needs to.

When I was a kid, Saturday-morning commercials held a lot of importance for me. They were like my church. Of course I watched the cartoons, too, but commercials seemed like the point. I loved commercials for girl toys like My Little Pony, Color Changing Sea Wees, and Strawberry Shortcake. I wanted to live in a girl toy commercial because everything looked so soft and welcoming. The girls in them always seemed kind and gentle, which was the opposite of how I experienced girls in real life. I would try to imitate the way they looked, brushing my hair until it shone, laughing gently, no sudden movements. Everything felt pastel-coloured, modern, and comforting. In real life, my parents preferred ruddy tones that evoked Fiestaware and court jesters.

Commercials for gender-neutral toys like Popples generally had a primary colour palette and more energizing music and featured children with brighter, more manic smiles. They would shriek and laugh in surprised delight. I would try these behaviours on, too, but they didn't feel as nice. And it didn't produce a good effect, either. I remember other kids exchanging looks.

Boy commercials absolutely did not do it for me. Their aggression stressed me out. The boys had sharp voices and rarely smiled, and the commercials always had a bleak colour palette: grey, brown, forest green, and black. I saw boys I knew adopt this way of behaving, and I stayed away from them.

My greatest success was in taking the girl toy personality into my everyday life. It made everything a lot easier. Being gentle lets you slide. Teachers, bus drivers, even other kids—kids who had bullied me in the past—they'd either smile or just let me go about my business. It was a huge relief. If there's nothing in your personality that creates friction, then the people who are looking for friction leave you alone. That was all I wanted.

At that time, I believed with my whole heart that I could recreate the idyllic world of toy commercials if I just bought those toys. My real world felt very different, and was full of floors that made your feet dirty and half-eaten loaves of dense, horrible ancient-grain bread. I wanted to live like a girl who drifted through the backyard in a pale blue smocked dress, making little impact, hardly making footprints in the grass. So I saved my allowance.

It worked, for a little bit. I would buy a Color-Changing Sea Wee; I'd open the package, smell the clean plastic, and all the dirty floors and old bread would fall away. I'd be in the Sea Wee's world.

But then, after a little while, the brilliance of the new toy would throw the rest of my life into stark comparison. Everything else in my house—my clothes, my parents, my other toys—would seem even more dank and pathetic.

And then, over time, the Color-Changing Sea Wee, or the My Little Pony, or whatever it was, absorbed the colour and texture of the rest of my life: grimy and dull. And even though you could supposedly bring it in the bath, after you did, it smelled like mildew.

We won the Lumber Board pitch. And as I hoped, my boss made me the strategy lead on the account. It is exciting to work on a project that actually matters. Maybe I can take a day off to walk in the forest and call it research. But what I have to do now is write an insight. In advertising, an insight is a singular thought that a team will develop creative against. It must convey a deep understanding of the brand, the audience the brand is talking to, and the culture that impacts both. It must also, for the creative team, feel like an emotional truth. It's the hardest part of my job, but it's also the most fulfilling. Writing a great insight was what got me on *Advertising Magazine*'s list.

Of course, my dead stalker turned up at my first Lumber Board meeting. He sat at the head of the table and made the room extremely cold.

He moved his mouth as though he was speaking and made motions of opening files, shuffling papers, and pulling out his phone. It felt like watching a mime. He never, ever looked at me. He seemed very careful.

Everybody else pretended they couldn't see him, but nobody took his seat.

Among people who work in advertising, accounts for things like lumber have a bad reputation. They mistakenly think that work for a raw material everyone already needs and uses won't require thoughtful insight or groundbreaking creative. What emotional relationship will the audience build with a plank? In the audit I'm doing, most of the ads I've found don't look beyond the functional:

- Hardness, strength, toughness, stiffness
- Mixed grain to tight grain
- Takes a stain well, takes paint well

But if you look only at your functional relationship to anything, it gets boring. Even things you adore. If I made an ad for boyfriends and described only the pragmatic relationship we have to them, it might say:

- Reaches for things on high shelves
- Has sex with you
- Will check to see if you need anything at the store

None of these things tell you why you have a romantic relationship. It's always the way someone changes your world that you fall in love with. And people really struggle when they try to describe that change. They might say, "There's just something about them." An insight is when you discover, isolate, and find the words for that something.

A functional ad for a Color-Changing Sea Wee might go something like this:

- Made of durable PVC plastic that won't break
- Changes colour underwater to entertain a child
- Brushable hair keeps child occupied in the act of detangling

Ads for children's toys actually used to sound like this because they were made for parents. If you're buying toys without an emotional investment in them, that information covers what you need to know. But things changed when someone discovered that if you create a whole world around a toy, then the child will get excited. They get excited because being a child is lonely and frustrating, and children lack control over much except the world they can create in their heads. And if you, the advertiser, can make your toy a passage to that world, you can sell pretty much anything.

At least that's the way it was for me.

I think there's a whole universe of things we haven't said about lumber. Lumber comes from trees, trees have souls, and souls are energy. *Lumber* has energy. I can feel it when I run my hand across the top of a table.

Actually, I don't think "lumber" is the right word.

"Lumber" is a word invented to take you away from the essence of the thing it describes. "Lumber" is a product, it's a component. A tree is wood. A table is a piece of a tree that stays in your house and never dies. Lumber is industrial, machine-made. Lumber ceases to exist as soon as it becomes something you love. We call it lumber to commodify it, but when it's in our home, it's wood.

It's not "lumber," it's wood.

This account will fill up with the best, most understated people at the agency. People content to be sitting and thinking about trees. That eliminates anyone who's chasing glamour or is too impressed with their own ideas. So far, I've chosen my colleague who wore the jumpsuit, a creative team of two forty-five-year-olds who share boxes of blue hair dye, and another account lead of an indeterminate age who has a calming presence, wears a lot of leather vests, and has dirty fingernails. You never see dirty fingernails at an ad agency, it's refreshing.

Our first assignment is a launch campaign to introduce the Lumber Board's (or should we start calling it the Wood Board's?) new brand to the nation. We have to make the campaign huge and impactful; I'm imagining TV, billboards, cinema ads, posters, influencer partnerships, and events.

I didn't go into work today. I texted my boss and told him I was OOO for research. He texted back *np*. It makes no difference to him; he's in Atlanta on King Koffee business. He's probably living it up at that old CEO's mansion.

I drove out of the city to a patch of forest at the end of the street my childhood best friend used to live on. It's not a conservation area, just a bit of land in the suburbs that hasn't been developed yet, which is rare. As children, my best friend and I would go into that forest and collect bugs in Tupperware containers. We'd bring them back home and watch them fight. I used to think *These bugs are enemies*. But now I realize they felt panicked and trapped and probably wouldn't have fought if they weren't forced to fit in a container together. You never see bugs fighting outside of Tupperware.

My childhood best friend doesn't live on this street anymore. We lost touch after we hit our early teens, but the forest remains there. It's jarring, after driving through all the suburban streets edged with the same houses and cars, to come to one that ends in tall dark trees. No wonder we spent so much time here.

It was quiet in the way only a forest is. Not silent like a recording studio; a forest quiet is a mix of sounds so natural that your ear just melts right into them and they become part of the sounds in your body.

Today, I walked among the trees that had known me when I was a child, and they felt the same now as they did then. I imagined having a hamper made of one of these trees, and it was a comforting idea.

Walking on the sun-dappled path, I came across a used condom. It didn't seem as gross as it would on a city sidewalk, and I asked myself why. I looked at it for a while. The latex had gotten yellow, like old paper. I found myself imagining bodies in the act of having sex, these familiar trees watching, the wind blowing through their leaves dampening the sound of lovers' grunts.

Sometimes it helps me to think of what an insight might have been for a piece of work I've loved. For instance, an insight for Irish Spring might have read: *We've all felt hopeless and beaten down by our day, then had a shower that revitalized us and made us new.* It seems like a fairly obvious statement, but that's exactly what an insight should confirm. It should feel like something you've known all along, but forgotten. If it feels like too much of a leap, your audience won't get it. They don't want to work too hard to have to understand a commercial. Remember, for soap it used to be "fits in the palm of your hand" and "reduces 10% more bad odours." In my career, I've found that it can take a lot of research and multiple attempts to think about something mundane in a new way.

Right now, in my notebook, there's a new page with this written at the top: *wood is a living thing and we take that for granted.* That was what kept running through my head as I left the forest at the end of my former best friend's street.

The Senior Talent Acquisition Officer with the pink hair dyed her hair seafoam green. It looks nice. When I complimented the change, she told me the pink was two hairs ago, and we need to see each other more often. So she's been stopping by my desk a lot. She'll bring a bottle of wine and two glasses. She'll ask me how I'm fitting in, then listen while I talk and pretend to drink. I've felt self-conscious about drinking ever since I drank that tequila.

She drinks the whole bottle, and doesn't seem to notice that I don't. It turns out she's pretty unhappy with the agency, too. She said the partners asked her to recruit more people who challenge the status quo, but when she started doing that, she discovered they don't actually want the status quo challenged. I believe that.

She wants to start a women's committee at the agency. She wants me to join it. The idea is we'd meet with the partners once a month and try to improve things for women here; get more women in leadership positions, for example. I admire her ambition, but it sounds exhausting. It's always exhausting when you're trying to get someone to do something they're lying about wanting to do.

What would you change if you could? she asked me. I told her we should get free pregnancy tests in the washrooms. She nodded very seriously and wrote it down. *These are the changes we need to make*, she said. I felt bad for both of us. She's trying to do something to make our agency better, and I've lost all hope that it can change. We're not a very effective duo. All I want to do is work on my wood project and look at hampers online.

The last time she stopped by, I caught my stalker peering up over the partition. All I could see were his eyes and his forehead. He was watching us. She saw him, too. *You hear all about these ghosts all the time, but you never see them,* she said. *I see him all the time, he's been following me everywhere,* I told her. *Be careful,* she said.

I presented my insight about wood as a living thing to the clients, and we had a really good discussion. They're aligned with the general direction. They didn't love it as much as I hoped they would. They want me to go deeper.

My stalker was not there. I don't know why. He must have known about the meeting, since he knows about every meeting. When I walked the clients out afterwards, I found myself looking for him. That's probably not healthy behaviour for me.

When I got back to my desk, I found an old issue of *Teen* on top of all my stuff. There was a sticky note stuck to the cover that said *thought you might find this interesting*. It was written in cursive with a rollerball pen. The cover story was "How to Flirt with a Guy, Even if You're Super Shy."

When I opened my desk drawer, my deodorant was missing.

After I hadn't seen him at the client meeting, it was almost a relief. Keep your friends close but your ghost stalkers closer, etc.

Today I finally have my appointment to see *Wash Up, Lasses!*

It's in the cave, and going down there makes me nervous. What message will it send to my stalker when he sees me? Will he be able to see me? Will I be able to see him?

There's only one elevator in the entire ad agency. It's 200 years old and very slow. It was the first elevator ever installed in the city. At that time, the agency was known for innovation and early adoption of the latest technologies. It was contemporary and relevant. Because of this heritage, the partners wanted to make the elevator an experience, not just a way to get between floors. Unfortunately, we still have to go between floors, and this elevator is very slow. On each floor, the elevator doors look different, representing different schools of design. On the eighth floor, which is modern and sleek, the doors are a teal glass that slide open with a whoosh. On the first floor, which was built before anything else, and which has an Industrial Revolution feel, there's a heavy folding iron gate. On my floor, it's inconspicuous-looking chrome and square light-up buttons. My floor was built in the 1980s.

The car itself is a mesh cage with a hardwood floor. Soft, worn dips in the wood are evidence of many years of feet. Hanging on the wall is a portrait of Julius Julius with a laurel wreath around his head. To make the elevator go up and down, you have to turn a crank. The crank takes a lot of arm strength, which I have not yet built because I take the stairs. There are stories of people starting here weak, then getting totally ripped by the time they leave.

Getting to the cave on the elevator takes about half an hour. Between floors, the elevator shaft is dark and graffitied, until you go below G (for ground). After G, you begin your descent into the cave. The walls drip, and they're crawling with those white millipedes. Sound gets muffled and drops out completely when you're going through parts of the cave where the limestone is porous. The smell of the air changes.

When you reach the bottom, the doors open onto a wall. In front of the wall, you'll find a little cart shaped like a 1970s Maserati Ghibli (Maserati is still one of our clients), and you ride a tiny railway through a tunnel while the car radio plays the Bee Gees. The headlights are the only lights.

It took thirty-four minutes to get to the cave, even with my strongest cranking. The ride in the Ghibli, which I've enjoyed in the past, stressed me out. Much darker than I remember. The battery in the headlights must have been low, because I could only see about two feet in front of me. I kept sensing shapes moving in the dark, and I kept feeling someone in the car with me, even though there was no one. It occurred to me that my stalker could just manifest in the passenger seat, and then what would I do?

The archivist sat at her desk wearing a blue silk wrap dress with gold chains rippling over her collarbones. She chatted with a junior creative team checking out twelve albums of recordings of Coke cans and bottles opening, dating back to 1892. They'd probably just received the brand as an assignment, because they looked so young and optimistic.

The archivist's desk was surrounded by life-sized, undefined, grey humanoid sculptures; the hands looked like mittens, and they had no faces. They all struck poses of distress: running, crouching, or shielding their heads. *She moved all these down here, aren't they terrifying?* The archivist told me they were from a fire safety campaign. They were created by our agency teams to remind people of Pompeii and installed in the charred ruins of a burnt-out apartment building downtown. If you scanned a code nearby, you'd get taken to a landing page with fire prevention tips.

To sign out *Wash Up, Lasses!* you have to provide a credit card, last year's tax return, and your bank manager's home phone number. *Wash Up* is very fragile and valuable. Normally, you sign for it and someone will go deep in the archives and get it for you, and then you have to sit at a fluorescent-lit desk and look at it under supervision.

But because the archivist is my friend, I was allowed to go with her to get it. The tunnels of the archives stretch for miles. If you stand at the mouth, which is the reception desk, you can't see to the end. The further you walk, the further back in time you go. The walls are lined with filing cabinets, above which are pasted notable posters and billboards. It's sparsely but warmly lit. As we walked toward the 1850s, the sounds of our footsteps and voices bounced and enveloped us. I felt peaceful in a way I hadn't in a long time. The archivist said, *It's because you're deeper in the earth, and your body recognizes its ultimate home.*

Passing through the 1980s, I saw a billboard of a bloody Ked sneaker on a road, ambulance lights fuzzy in the distance. Underneath was the line *Don't drink and drive.* It's interesting to remember that there was a time when you had to tell people; the ad campaign had not yet been conceived when they were growing up. In the 1950s, we passed a massive image of a smiling woman, her head tilted back, unafraid to show her teeth because her toothpaste kept them white. In the 1890s, a framed print ad for Coca-Cola told the reader that the drink would relieve the fatigue that comes from *over-work, over-shopping, or over-play, putting vim into tired brains and bodies for just 5 cents.* Coke wasn't an intentionally culture-building brand at its outset.

When we got to the 1850s, the time of the Crimean War and *Wash Up, Lasses!*, the walls were decorated with wheatpaste posters for Owl Brand Cigars. Owl Brand was a client of the agency until they went bankrupt in 1931, when the preference for Cuban cigars surged. We came to a black steel vault embedded in the stone wall. The archivist told me the steel vault is as much a part of the agency's history as the work inside it. Apparently, in the 1920s, an executive assistant accidentally locked herself inside it and died. Someone sent her to pull out a document for one of the partners, and everyone was in such a work frenzy that no one noticed how long she'd been gone. She suffocated before anyone thought to go down and look for her. I asked the archivist how many people had died in the agency. *Oh dozens*, she said, *maybe hundreds.*

She unlocked two sets of iron gates, and together we spun two giant wheels on an iron door that I learned weighed twenty-five tons. When the door opened, there was another iron gate to unlock.

We stepped inside and motion detector lights in the vault flipped on, surprisingly golden. Franz Liszt played through a speaker system embedded in the ceiling. *Very popular during the Crimean War*, the archivist said. I noticed a black-and-white photo portrait of a young, smiling woman with wavy bobbed hair and small teeth. The receptionist bowed her head and made the sign of the cross. *That was the woman who died in here. I hope she lost consciousness before she figured out no one was coming for her*, she said.

The first thing I noticed about *Wash Up, Lasses!* was the smell: pulpy, watery, a bit metallic. When the archivist removed it from its protective envelope, the air filled with particles. They'd travelled all the way from 1850 to up my nose. They coated my fingers.

The illustration is incredible. The women's bodies are plump and curvaceous, their flesh spilling out of their ripped linen dresses. Their breasts are almost entirely exposed, except for taut strips of dirty fabric covering aggressively perky nipples. Their asses are huge, perfect round peaches that no skirt could cover modestly, particularly not the filmy skirts the illustrator drew for them.

I've been staring at the mimeograph for months now, but what doesn't come through in that copy is the women's expressions. They're in anguish, but the corners of their mouths are twitched up. If you're just walking by quickly, as I imagine people would have when the posters were up, the women look like they're smiling. But they're not, not really. In the background of the image, behind a barrel, there's a desperate, sick-looking man crawling toward them, as if using his very last breaths to get closer. He's in sexual agony, drooling and reaching out. One of the lasses has noticed him. Her bosom is heaving, and you can tell she's terrified, but her face invites him closer. It's an expression that perfectly captures the fear and mania of being desired.

The disease itself is represented by cross-hatched patches, blotches of goop, and stink lines. It's thriving.

It really does make you want to wash your hands, doesn't it? the archivist asked, offering me an acid-free wet wipe. I said it did, and wiped my hands.

When I got back to my desk, I found the longest email yet from my stalker:

Last night I dreamt a most compelling dream. I was sitting in an expansive and populous cafeteria drinking a salty, oever steeped tea with nothing to sweeten its flavour on the table. I began my search for a bit of honey or something of the like when I spotted you, standing by a bowl of sugar cubes. I took your hands. You had the most agreeable little fingertips.

Cosa significa? 😁

I read it to the archivist, and she said, *That is disgusting,* then took a long drag of her cigarette and said, *He thinks he is being romantic,* and she laughed, exhaling smoke in short bursts. *What if you stuck your agreeable little fingertips down his throat and choked him? I hope he dies.*

He's dead, I said.

Not dead enough, said the archivist.

I would not describe my fingers as agreeable. They're not terrible, they're just regular. A regular length and width. The lines on my knuckles remind me of knee pads. I rarely get manicures, and I've never successfully grown long nails. People have told me my hands feel soft, but I think they're talking about the backs of my hands, not my fingers.

I've seen beautiful fingers. Jennifer O'Neill in the 1978 ad for Cutex Creme Enamel, those are beautiful fingers. I wouldn't say I've ever seen agreeable fingers, though, except on dolls, or possibly babies.

Actually, the fingers on the women in *Wash Up, Lasses!* are agreeable. Mostly, the way the lasses are rendered is lascivious, all swooping curves and spilling wild breasts, but they do have these soft, pliable little hands.

I was sitting at my desk, working. All the other people in my department had gone to lunch. I felt cold breath on the top of my head.

Don't look up, said a voice. I didn't look up; I could tell it was him. He was hanging over the top of the partition, breathing down on me.

I hadn't heard him speak before. His voice was a combination of a whisper and a growl. I stopped typing. I froze.

Into the top of my head, he whispered, *I mourn for the man I could have been if I'd had a good woman by my side.*

I could feel his lips brushing the hairs that stick up from my hairline. They felt cold, like a corpse lying in a morgue, or Jell-O that's sat in the fridge overnight.

I left work early, took a cab home, then took a very hot shower that steamed up the windows and mirrors. I took the shower that women in horror movies get murdered in. And I scrubbed. Normally, I'm quite cautious with my skin, I don't like to cause micro-abrasions, but this was the first time he'd touched me. I washed my hair, but I could still feel his corpse lips on the top of my head.

I took that bar of Irish Spring, slick from the steam, and I went to town. I haven't used a commercial soap in years, I'd forgotten how exquisitely they lather. Artisan soap just doesn't generate the same bubbles. The smell was so strong and fresh. It made me sneeze. I have not washed my hair with soap since I was fifteen. It's a completely different experience. I lathered all through my hair and rinsed. I lathered again and rinsed, massaging my scalp with my fingertips. I lathered a third time and there were bubbles falling off my head in heaps and I couldn't stop sneezing. I felt my hair squeak between my fingers. That meant I had stripped out all the natural oils.

I rubbed the soap over every part of my body over and over again, between my toes and behind my ears. I covered myself in foam.

I imagined I was the miner in the commercial—hopeless, exhausted, and filthy, then clean and reborn. I scrubbed and lathered until I was red and raw and the bar of Irish Spring shrank to a tiny sliver with sharp edges, then I rubbed the sliver between my hands until it disappeared and I watched the last bubbles swirl down the drain.

That night I dreamed about the forest at the end of my childhood best friend's street. In the dream, we'd gone to the mall. We each had bags full of floral scoop-neck tees. We had turned thirteen: the year I stopped answering her texts. We walked down the forest path, the sun bouncing off her white sneakers. The birds sang and hopped from tree to tree, and soft red mushrooms grew from the dirt. She told me that her school cafeteria would get a Taco Bell next September. I told her I was jealous but, secretly, I felt happy for her. They'd probably bring in cute boys to work at the Taco Bell.

When I woke up, I felt peaceful.

I wrote down some thoughts in a notebook I keep beside my bed:

- Trees are probably the first non-human living things we see: on the drive home from the hospital after we're born, we probably see trees.
- Wherever there are trees, there's a network of tree roots.
  - Trees in the forest are all related: their roots grow together, they're a family.
  - Then—does that mean all trees are one living being, actually? Rather than a lot of separate individual trees, are they one thing?
  - Because I eat food that grows from the earth, where trees grow, and that is fertilized by their fallen leaves, am I part tree?
- We use a lot of "tree" language when we're talking about establishing a sense of home:
  - Laying down roots
  - Somewhere I can branch out
  - Family tree
- Every year, a tree goes through a human lifetime: spring is childhood, summer is adulthood, fall is aging, winter is death.

I can't get the words quite right, but there's an insight in there, somewhere.

Taco Bell was founded by a white man who owned a hot dog stand across the street from a Mexican restaurant. When he saw the long lines at the Mexican restaurant, he decided he needed to sell tacos, not hot dogs. He started selling tacos but couldn't get the recipe quite right. His neighbours across the street invited him over and showed him how it was done. He opened his first restaurant in 1962, and five years later, he had 100 Taco Bells. The owners of the restaurant whose tacos he copied still own only one restaurant, but it's considered an institution.

During the Crimean War, when the *Wash Up, Lasses!* campaign launched, nobody knew that a virus was just a living thing trying to survive. They didn't know that it doesn't have bad intentions toward people, that we're just the soft, permeable, damp, mucous-y carrier that is perfect for its survival. A human body is a million different habitats perfect for making life, and we hug each other and kiss and sleep together, so if you're a virus looking to make a move, you can hop from one of us to another easily. You can travel; you can grow your population.

For human beings to survive, we have to behave like a virus does with respect to other living things. For instance, we attack and destroy whole communities of trees and make our houses out of them. That's all a virus does: attack and destroy us and make us its home. A person isn't better than a virus or any other thing that's alive.

Washing up obliterates communities of bacteria and germs, including ones we've lived in peace with for millennia. Washing up leaves behind nothing, just the feeling of clean, which is a feeling of absence.

Clean is a space to fill, a fresh start. Clean is momentary; you can't maintain it. As soon as you are clean, you start to get dirty again. Just like how as soon as you are born, you begin to die.

I stopped texting my childhood best friend because after I'd gotten out of the hospital for anorexia when I was thirteen, I met a guy. He was the most beautiful teenager in town, a skateboarder who worked at the record store and had long hair. Everyone fell in love with him, but he liked me. We dated for four weeks and made out on his parents' couch. I'd been perceived as an anonymous twerp all my life, but suddenly everyone knew who I was and thought I was pretty. Other guys started to talk to me, which had never happened before.

He broke up with me because I cried one night after he stood me up. Well, he didn't break up with me, his friend did it for him. I felt like nothing after that, and my anorexia came back with a vengeance. Then, instead of everyone thinking I was pretty, everyone knew me as the dumped anorexic.

A cool girl my age whose parents had kicked her out of the house got an apartment in town, and she asked me to move in with her. I needed very badly to escape my personality, and it was obvious that having my own apartment was a much better way to achieve fame than being lonely or having an eating disorder. I was tired of pity. The cool girl and I moved in, and I traded my anorexia for drugs, which, it turned out, were the same thing, anyway.

Years later, I would miss my childhood best friend, but she moved on with her life in a functional, productive way, studying science and eventually getting a job as an entomologist. She married a man, and they had two babies.

I wonder if the *Wash Up, Lasses!* poster still has germs on it. How could it not be coated in them? Those posters were plastered all over hospital walls, in bathrooms, and in public areas in infected neighbourhoods.

People would have sneezed on them, or felt faint and leaned on them, or coughed and wiped their hands on them. Kleenex wasn't introduced to the Western world until 1924. How long do germs live?

Lately, I hate thinking of the archivist down in that damp cave with her arthritis, those germy posters, and my stalker's ghost. I know she's tough, but you don't live an entire life just to get bats stuck in your hair during your golden years.

On our last cigarette break, she told me she was political when she was young, in Rome. When she was seventeen, the archivist was raped. It was common for victims to marry their rapists because, back then, the rapist could avoid going to jail since, according to the law, a man could not technically rape his wife. The archivist turned down her rapist's proposal.

Her refusal made huge news in Rome, and women old and young who had married their rapists began to question whether or not they'd had to do so. Militias of local women began keeping vigil at the archivist's house, because she'd received death threats and bricks through the window.

Her rapist hung himself in a public piazza and became, briefly, a sympathetic character. But the archivist went to the press and told them that as a young girl, she'd always dreamed of marrying a man who would be a kind and gentle father, who would help her build a home where love bounced off the walls. In her statement, she said she knew that anyone capable of rape could never be that man.

The best communications strategy, the archivist told me, *is the truth*.

The archivist did fall in love with a kind and gentle man, eventually. Her family gave him a career at the agency, and he did well. They moved to Canada, went to restaurants, and shopped on the weekends. They had a baby girl, and love did bounce off the walls of their home. They used to read together on a plush leather sofa in the evenings. He'd make oatmeal with cinnamon for breakfast. She said that these were some of the calmest, happiest years of her life, until he was hit by a car and killed.

Her family had given her a job, also. She was an account director. But after her husband died, she kept showing up to work drunk, and the clients noticed. They moved her around from account to account, department to department, until she finally requested that she go to the archives, so she wouldn't have to see anyone.

She might still show up to work drunk, I can't tell. Some people manage to perform a very elegant version of alcoholism.

This morning, I woke up, opened my notebook, and found this in my notes:

INSIGHT LINES!

- There would be no disease if we didn't need each other.
- There would be no filth for disease to thrive in if we didn't need to be near each other.
- There would be no love if there was no death to fear. This is why we need to be near each other, so we can spread disease and kill one another.

It's in my stalker's handwriting. It's very upsetting, and they're not even good insights.

When I went to the bathroom and blew my nose, the snot came out grey. I must still have poster particles up there.

I got a ping on my phone at 4 a.m. and saw an email from my stalker glowing on the screen. I sat up in bed. The room was freezing. The email read:

You are young and sweet and inexperienced; I have not approached you for fear that I would mess up your life. Forever, I've meant to tell you. Now, I'm telling you.

I put the phone back on the nightstand and tried to go back to sleep. Half an hour later, I got another email:

For a long time, I've lived in the dark, but now I believe I deserve some light and kindness FOR ONECE. So I'm telling you my emotions, just spitting them at your feet.

I turned off the sound notifications, but I couldn't make myself close my eyes. I lay back down and tried unsuccessfully to unclench my jaw. The phone lit up with another email that just read:

What a relief for me!

The emails kept coming every few minutes, one after another, and my room got so cold I could see my breath.

4:53 a.m.:

Do I wish I had confessed sooner? Perhaps, my lamb. But this postponed eruption feels revelatory.

5:01 a.m.:

You mustnt be shocked, you are very perceptive and have perhaps always felt my emotions yanking at you.

5:17 a.m.:

Now that I've gotten to know you, I can see you are as winsome and angeliquw as I perceived.

And finally, at 5:45 a.m.:

I will mix you a cocktail. Not too strong hehe.

The sun had begun coming through the blinds. I texted my boss that I felt sick and wasn't able to come in to work. I pulled the covers over my head and made a little tent. The next time the phone screen lit up, it was a text from my boss that read *np*.

The landlord of our teenager apartment would drill holes in our bedroom wall. He used them to watch us change. When we found them, we'd cover them up with gum, but new ones kept getting drilled. The bedroom began to smell like Doublemint.

To pay my rent, I worked at a restaurant. To do this, I had to drop out of high school. I kept trying to go back, but on my last try, the principal took me into his office and said, *You know what? It seems like maybe now isn't the right time for you to be in high school. It seems like you've got other things going on.*

It was true: I did have other things going on. But I don't know what the right time for me to be in high school was if it wasn't when I was a teenager. I never graduated. I got evicted after my landlord realized that I would never "come over" to his place and "smoke a joint"—a.k.a. get roofied via a cup of mint tea and molested on the couch while unconscious.

I'd heard the stories.

I worked at the restaurant until I was old enough to work at a bar.

One night at the bar, I got into a conversation about the revival of Gothic style with a man who was the creative director of an ad agency. He asked me to come in for an interview because he liked the way I thought about culture. During the interview, he played with a Rubik's Cube. He asked me what bourbon I liked. Fortunately, because of the bar, I had an answer. A few weeks later, he offered me my first agency job. I never thought I would have a job somewhere nice, but it's been ten years since that interview and now I'm "The Thoughtful Maverick."

The seafoam-green-haired HR woman gave me my six-month performance review. I'm supposed to work on seeing myself as a leader and not act so grateful when other people give me their time. I'm supposed to lean forward when I talk and make eye contact with each person at the table.

I told her the review felt gendered, and she said, *I say similar things to a lot of young women, but this does apply to you.* I asked her if there was anything about my actual work. She said, *I'll have to go back and check.*

Great, I said.

I texted my boss and told him that I'd work from home for the rest of the day. *np,* he texted back, then, two minutes later, *thx.*

I found my hamper! I can't believe it. I walked home from work today for the first time in a while. The air had that beautiful, golden, humid quality. I did something I never do and stopped into stores along the way. I chatted with shopkeepers and looked at things. I walked into an antique store, a place I must have passed hundreds of times. There it was: the Ananas hamper. Well, it was a big woven basket in the shape of a pineapple, anyway. The man who owned the store told me that this particular style achieved popularity in the 1940s and that it was made by (probably long-dead) authentic craftsmen. He told me that he comes across them every so often and always buys them because people love them. I put down my credit card and told him I'd been looking for a hamper like this forever. When he rang up the total, it was a lot less than the one I'd pined for online. I told him about the site where I'd originally seen the Ananas Fair Trade Hamper, and how they donate 10% of sales to lunch programs for children of basket weavers. He asked me, *Do you know for sure that basket weavers want lunch programs for their children from people like us?* It was a good question.

An email from my stalker:
You're a high quality girl.

Biscotti had her puppies. They were born under my desk over the weekend. When I came into work on Monday, there were two executive assistants and a vet cleaning them off and checking their little hearts with stethoscopes. One of the assistants handed me the tiniest one and said, *She was born under your desk, you should name her.* Her head was so soft, and her ears were like satin. *We should call her Camilla*, I said. Camilla is the archivist's name.

Here's where I've landed with the Lumber Board insight:

- Wood has always supported us, literally. We have leaned against tree trunks, lain on floors, and collapsed our heads in our arms on tables.
- Wood is the first thing we turn to when we need to defend our soft bodies from the world. We hide behind trees, use wood to make the frames of our houses, and made the first shields used in battle out of wood.
- When we're born, we're placed in wooden cradles. When we die, we're placed in wooden coffins. Wood welcomes us into the world, and it melts with us as we return to the dirt.

I think those are some of the best insight lines I've written. I'm very optimistic about making the list next year.

I

II *The Creative Director*

There's a famous image of the boy. It shows him smiling, proud and handsome, standing on a pile of limestone rubble with a sledgehammer over his shoulder. He has been the face of the National Lime and Chemical Company for decades. That was my doing. The line I wrote to accompany the photo was "Strong foundations help us grow." It's been the NL & CC's tag line for fifty-two years and counting.

This is the boy whose body is buried in the cave at Julius Julius. We knew each other before I became a copywriter. We were general labourers, building the agency's elevator. It was our first job. It was everyone's first job, because we were all fourteen years old.

I was deflated by the realization, about midway through my career, that it was my most boring work that had staying power.

I shouldn't say boring; I'll say "pragmatic." It certainly paid the bills, writing all those pragmatic lines.

Besides, this tag line has sentimental value. It was the first one I wrote that was used in a national campaign, and it sits forever under a picture of my childhood friend.

"Strong foundations help us grow" has multiple meanings. The first is that buildings that rest on strong foundations grow into the sky. That's obvious. The second, implied meaning is that strong foundations allow workers to grow and, by extension, the economy and, by an even further extension, the country.

The boy is still on pamphlets, posters, and billboards all over the country. He is my ghost, and he haunts me. I hope people are curious about his identity; I hope he's not just part of the ad wallpaper they try to ignore every day.

I think a good tag line is a little poem, animating people's imaginations about the brand it represents, giving it new dimensions, like a diamond. It should stick in a person's brain and tell them something. The more a tag line sticks, the more it should tell them.

As a crushed aggregate, limestone makes a very strong and durable foundation. In its original form, of course, limestone is porous, permeable, and prone to crumbling.

Julius Julius is built on top of a network of limestone caves. One day, a sinkhole is supposed to open and swallow the whole place into the earth.

When you're assigned to an account, you become an expert in your clients' industries. It can be a lot of fun. I was the head copywriter on our work for the Polish company Krupnik Honey Liqueur. An interesting fact: the first honey liquor is said to have been created by Hippocrates, who used it to cure intestinal worms. Of course, by the time I got to Krupnik, the primary audience was housewives who entertained.

I created a series of cocktails that I named after Polish luminaries. The recipes were published as tear-out pages in *Milady's Evening Reader.* My favourite was Fahrenheit's Flame:

3 OUNCES KRUPNIK HONEY LIQUEUR

1 OUNCE TRIPLE SEC

1 OUNCE GOOSEBERRY JUICE

1 OUNCE CHERRY JUICE

SPLASH OF PIOŁUNÓWKA
(POLISH ABSINTHE-LIKE LIQUEUR)

1 TEASPOON EACH RED AND WHITE CURRANTS,
CHOPPED VERY FINELY, FOR GARNISH

Serve over ice, sprinkling the currants on top.

Place of origin is so important for a liqueur. People feel destabilized when they drink, and it's comforting for them to remember they're imbibing in the company of nations.

I was also the copywriter on King Koffee. That assignment was wonderful. I travelled to the company headquarters in Atlanta, of course, but I also got to visit Costa Rica, where the beans are harvested by coffee pickers up in the cloudy mountains. Sometimes many generations of a family will harvest the same land over centuries. Coffee beans begin life nestled inside bright little red fruits called coffee cherries. I think about this whenever I drink a cup.

Some of my colleagues don't like to travel for work, but I love not being at home. I've taken probably 150 trips to Richmond, Virginia, because the National Lime people are there. Nobody knows me in that city, so I visit a piano bar, go to a farm, anything. I love taking a break from being myself.

It's a good way to strengthen your creativity: doing something new every day. This can be difficult when work locks you into a routine, but I try to keep up the practice with small efforts, like visiting a new convenience store. If you live in a city, there are limitless options if you keep an open mind.

I was already considered an expert when I was assigned to the National Lime and Chemical Company account. Having been a general labourer was useful to the work and to the client relationship. I was salt of the earth, the partners liked to say. That means working class. The men of the NL & CC were also salt of the earth.

When I was a general labourer, my work was often simple. I'd spend whole days moving bones from one pile to another. Back then, we'd sing songs we'd learned in school while we worked. The whole crew knew the same ones, because there were a lot of us from Park Public.

When we were asked to run papers with measurements upstairs, I'd always volunteer, because it meant I got to go through all the wood-panelled hallways and pass the framed ads.

I remember an Old Gold cigarettes poster featuring Laurel and Hardy, smoking with serene, wealthy expressions on their faces. I remember the Flora-net hairnet girl, looking charmingly over her shoulder from the photo on the package, smiling and confident. I remember a tranquil mother and baby, rocking in a chair next to a radiator from the American Ideal Radiator Company, safe and warm despite the winter outside.

Everything I wanted for myself was on those walls.

Mostly, of course, we just swung our Estwing sledgehammers. Swinging those hammers was the job.

That would be what killed the boy.

Well, actually, it was a mistake the men in charge made about where to swing that killed him. I know now that these accidents are never the fault of the people who die in them.

Later, I'd get to know a lot of the men in charge. They were a disappointment. They would complete the tasks of the day, have the necessary conversations. I kept waiting for one of them to say something insightful or make a surprising business decision, but it just never happened.

There are men in charge who start wars and invent penicillin, but there are more men in charge who want to have a nice day, then go to bed. The latter are the ones who actually run the world, slowly chugging us on until we die.

The boy was handsome. People paid attention to him, and he made a good impression. In school, at the corner store, or walking through the alley with mud on his face, everyone was charmed. If he'd lived a little longer, he could have done anything he wanted; he could have been president of the company. But he didn't know that, being so young. He'd have rather been strong, or clever, or a fast runner.

I was a fast runner. It was my whole personality. I won all the races at school, took home all the ribbons. That's why people wanted to be my friend. I had accomplishments.

I started running because I couldn't sleep. Any little sound would wake me up. In The Precinct, the birds start singing before the sun rises, and that's when my eyes would rip open. I'd wake up with a pounding heart every morning, full of adrenaline.

I would run through the neighbourhood, the street dogs all around me, a little pack of bodies loping together.

My favourite was a blonde sausage dog with big brown eyes and long wavy ear fur.

When the sun is just rising in The Precinct, it's easy to forget what they say about our neighbourhood. The light is pink and gold, the vegetable gardens smell fresh and green, and no one is outside to frown at you just for being there.

Back when I started, it wasn't as common to see runners on the streets. People thought I was odd. Now there's lots of conversation about the benefits of running. Endorphins, mood regulation. That was what I got from the exercise, a bit of peace. I just didn't know the science at the time.

The boy was tall with broad shoulders, dark eyes, and an easy smile. Everyone in our class had loved him at one point or another. When he took a breath to speak, we'd all turn, each of us already knowing where he was in the room, even the teacher.

He had the sort of sweet, distracted way of being that makes a person easy to adore.

He never took advantage of all the attention. The love notes, the purposely forgotten barrettes, the lunch baskets filled with his favourite sandwiches: they all passed through his attention like sand through his fingers.

The boy took after his father, who used to be the star of our neighbourhood. Even the growling, scraggly-eared street dogs trusted him, so I did, too. He was gentle and used to feed the dogs dinner scraps. Once I saw him give my sausage dog a whole chicken breast. I'll bet it made her day.

Before the war, the boy's father had been a builder. He'd laid the foundation for the F&R Lazarus department store and the Colonial Bank block. He had even done repairs on the St. Monica's Church spire.

Cities are forever, he told me. *If you build in the city, you have eternal life.*

I understood what he meant when I started working. Your sweat drips onto the stone. You become part of the building, and generations of people live their lives in something you made for them. Even if they never know you, you're there.

But the boy's father came back from the war different. He was frightened, anxious, and easy to startle.

He couldn't work a job, or even complete a task around the little two-room house he shared with the boy and the rest of his family. A heavy step or a sneeze in the other room would make him jump.

So he'd let time trickle away on the back stoop, watching the rest of us wake, walk, go, and return.

The boy's father had been a sapper in the war, which is someone who digs tunnels under enemy camps. These tunnels would be filled with dynamite and then exploded when enemy soldiers were above.

Often the sappers would drill through walls of solid lime. But sometimes, if they couldn't risk making a lot of noise, they would paint the walls with vinegar and wait for the acid to melt the stone.

Didn't that take forever? we'd ask.

It did, but our pulses were racing the whole time, said the father.

Every so often, a sapper from the good side would encounter a sapper from the bad side while tunnelling underground.

In this situation, the two men had to fight to the death. The boy's father told us that when it happened to him, he had to beat the other guy with the butt of a gun that wouldn't fire.

He dragged his enemy's body to the surface in case he could be sent home for burial. He saw that the man was still breathing, but very, very low. He laid him out and made him as comfortable as possible. Moments later, the dynamite the boy's father had laid detonated, and the ground blew up underneath the low-breathing man.

The ad appeared in the Sunday-afternoon paper:

MAKE HISTORY

JULIUS JULIUS
The Advertising, Art & Copy Agency

Seeks strong men to become builders
of the future in the construction of
the city's first elevator.

Learn a trade and become master
of a professional specialty that
will be in demand.

Wednesday morning, apply within.

We'll choose the best.

The boy found his father on the stoop, sat down next to him, and read the ad aloud.

I'm old enough to work, and I'd like to, the boy said.

The father put his hand on the boy's shoulder. For the first time in months, the hand felt heavy and steady.

We assumed our youth would put us at a disadvantage, that bigger, stronger men would be the preference. But the boy believed he was uniquely qualified. He imagined marching up to the men in charge and saying, *Look here, my father was a builder in the city and a sapper in the war! Tunnels are in my blood!*

And the men in charge would nod and say, *Tunnels are in his blood, it's true. And what is an elevator but a tunnel standing on its end?*

And then he would get the job. They wouldn't even ask his age.

As the boy was falling asleep, he imagined his father sitting in the dark, a shadow painting vinegar on bright white limestone, willing it to melt while men bled to death on the ground above his head, soaking the soil.

In the morning, the boy, his father, and I walked to Julius Julius. Our sausage dog came with us.

The line was long. There were older men holding tool kits they owned in experienced hands, and there were boys like us, looking for a start. There were men who had just come to the city, and others with generations of their family buried at St. Monica's.

We waited in that line for two hours.

A person's creative output is a map of their life. Everything I've written is part of me, even if I didn't want it to be. It took me a long time to realize this. Even if I was just writing a little thing for King Koffee, some element of my experience echoed through the work. I've seen things years later and thought, *Ah yes, I was going through a hard time when I wrote that tag line.*

If you've seen my work (much to my embarrassment, sometimes), you know me.

We were interviewed in groups of three. The boy, his father, and I were permitted to go in together.

We walked up hundreds of stairs to a big wood-panelled room with a vaulted glass ceiling. The sun shone all around and danced on the walls. That glass sparkled: they must have cleaned it every day.

At the far end, a frighteningly beautiful woman sat behind a desk.

Do approach, she chirped. She looked us up and down, gave a curt nod, gave the dog a pat on the head, then began the slow work of sliding open a heavy oak door that led to a different room. She refused our offers of help, despite the obvious physical strain.

We found ourselves standing in front of three impressive men with glossy beards and identical grey wool suits. I was aware of a stain on the pocket of my shirt.

The one in the middle spoke to the boy:

The work will be physical and the days will be long. This elevator will be a triumph, but it won't be easy. We want men who are fit for a challenge. You and the boy to your left are young, and the repetitive stress to your shoulder probably won't cause lasting damage.

Our shoulders are good, said the boy.

However, said the man, his beard gleaming, *the older fellow to your right—*

Oh, I'm not looking for work, interrupted the father. *I'm a guardian; this is my son and his school friend.*

That's good, said the impressive man. *Family is very important to us. We think of Julius Julius as a family. You're part of that now. You'll start Monday morning.*

We thanked the men.

I remember that the boy caught everyone, including himself, by surprise by bending in a deep, reverent bow. One of the impressive men giggled, and a little snot bubble blew up at the gateway to his nose.

On Monday morning, we learned that everyone chosen to build the elevator was our age. We were boisterous, it felt like a school party. We were wrong to have thought they'd want bigger, stronger men. It was just us.

I've since learned this: adding an elevator to a building does not need to be complicated. It requires basic understanding of the building's geography and, if tunnelling below, as we were, an understanding of the kind of ground upon which the building is standing. That last part is critical.

At the time, there were no other elevators in the city. But there were other elevators in the world. Earlier in the year, the partners at Julius Julius had assembled an elevator advisory board. They'd consulted with some of the world's top builders.

That board had spoken to experienced elevator people on four continents, including those responsible for the holy dumbwaiter at Saint Catherine's Monastery in Sinai, Egypt, and the men who installed the hardy lift at Potbelly Sandwich Shop in Washington, DC.

The thought was that maybe those elevator builders could come to Julius Julius and oversee the project, to ensure that all involved were in good hands.

What the advisory board quickly discovered was that the experts wanted money.

A discussion was had among the partners. The ideal option would be to hire an expert and a seasoned crew. But profits had not been as large as expected that year. A plan B was needed.

Besides, weren't some of the top creative and logistical minds already working for Julius Julius? And while the owners of those minds had not specifically built or ridden elevators, wasn't it just a simple rope-and-pulley system? And hadn't elevators originated in ancient Rome to lift rabid lions into the arena at the Colosseum? And wasn't the agency's founder, Julius Julius, himself an ancient Roman?

I've observed that if a person has lived a very smooth life, like the partners at Julius Julius typically have, they aren't readily able to see the complications they create for others. It's not their fault, since they are actually not able to perceive problems.

The men decided plan B would do. There was an art department at the agency staffed with talented draftsmen.

Well, the partners had assumed they were draftsmen because they worked at drafting tables. But, actually, they were illustrators. They drew the Flora-net hairnet girl and the lasses in *Wash Up, Lasses!*

Either way, they were talented visual thinkers. They would design the elevator, and our crew of boys would execute their plan.

The art department took daily strolls around the building. They assessed its structure, knocking on walls and observing corners.

They decided to remove an existing stairwell just off the entrance and replace it with a shaft in which would travel the elevator.

The seeming ease of this idea made everyone optimistic. The difficult part would be drilling down into the caves.

The network of caves under Julius Julius had been formed many years ago by ancient rivers. Most had dried up, but they had left a big, deep pond below the surface. The water was so clear that, if you shone a light into it, you could see the shrimp scuttling along the bottom, a mile down. It gave the place an ominous, energized feeling. I'd sometimes think I could smell the water, even though it was deep underground.

The caves were to be home to the agency's first archives. The archives served a great purpose. Their existence told the world that the work Julius Julius produced was worthy of keeping. It would correct the opinion that advertising was about making a quick, dishonest profit. It would make accessible to everyone the artistry, care, and insight that filled our days.

First, we demolished the stairwell. We began with three teams of two boys on each flight: top, middle, and bottom. We each got an Estwing sledgehammer, and we learned to swing them in time with one another.

We discovered the concrete was full of big rocks. We had to pry them free, then shove them off. On the very first day, one of the boys working on the bottom got clocked on the head by a tumbling rock. He was unconscious for five minutes. When he woke up, he spoke in gibberish. He was sent home. He never came back.

We devised a system. We'd all save our rocks until we got a pile, then the whole lot of us would push them off the side at once, yelling *rock!* so everyone knew to get out of the way.

Pulverizing the staircase took us about two months. The art directors decided the easiest thing to do with the rocks would be to break them down into sand, which was then put in buckets and taken down to the beach.

There's probably still some sand from the old Julius Julius stair-well down at that beach.

Estwing sledgehammers are made in Illinois by a company founded by a Swedish immigrant. I loved mine. It's still the most substantial thing I've ever touched. It made me feel powerful, even more so than my running medals.

The hammers are made of a single piece of tool steel and bound in leather. They have within them the language to tell a body how to move for complete impact. As soon as you hold one, you know what to do.

That is actually a line I once wrote for Estwing: *As soon as you hold one, you know what to do.*

Our little blonde sausage dog came to work with us every day. The whole crew fell in love with her. She'd get a spectacular feeding from all of us, walking down the line when our lunch boxes were open, a treat for her at every stop.

The boy called her Spaghetti because of her wavy yellow ears. Sometimes she brought a boyfriend, and we called him Macaroni, just to keep the theme going.

In the evening, Spaghetti and Macaroni would walk back home to The Precinct with us, and they'd fall asleep on one of our stoops until it was time to get up, go for a run, and do it all over again.

The boy's family got happier. His job lightened the mood in the house. His father would ask about the boy's day and offer tips. His mother would buzz around and kiss her husband on the temple. The boy gave his father money so his mother could get a Flora-net hairnet. The mother began buying orange packages of crackers and tins of tuna bearing illustrations of fishermen. There was more food and less worry.

The boy's father got a job at the library, shelving books.

He pushes the carts around, the boy said. *There are no loud noises to startle him. It's perfect.*

The boy's father had begun to resemble his former self. He broke into an easy smile when he spotted us coming down the street.

I was the first one to break the floor. The crack spread from my feet to the edges of the walls. Out of that crack came scuttling hundreds of white millipedes, panicked by the light. They ran over our shoes, up our pant legs, into the corners, into our hats, through our hair. I pulled one out of my ear and flung it against the wall before it could burrow any deeper.

I watched Spaghetti take a bite of one and spit it out. Its legs still quivered, even though it was just a severed half.

A jackhammer was procured, and the boy was chosen to operate it. It made the loudest sound I'd ever heard. The boy laughed as he used it, his entire body vibrating. He got through the floor so quickly he fell through.

We heard a splash, then a yell, then more splashing, then the boy's voice echoing in the dark.

I found the cave!

I'm okay!

We lowered a rope for him to climb up, and he was soaking wet with a leech stuck to his neck when he got to the top.

There's a pond down there, too!

There is carbonic acid in the cave's water. It's the same stuff that makes a bottle of Perrier fizzy. People sometimes say that their teeth feel especially clean after drinking a lot of Perrier, and that's because the carbonic acid erodes tooth enamel. Over the years, the water had eroded the limestone in the caves and made the walls weak. This is something an expert might have known, but we didn't.

The photographer came the day after the boy fell through the floor to document the historic work being done.

Initially, the boy was instructed to pose with the jackhammer, but the tool was too big. It overpowered him visually and made him look like a child.

For his second pose, the boy was instructed to hold his sledgehammer over his shoulder and stand on the rocks. That's the photo that we'd use for the NL & CC advertisement. It was perfect; he looked dazzling in his potential.

I remember the photographer being especially taken with him.

I remember the men at the top calling him their best worker, even though we all worked the same.

I remember him being very agreeable, taking delight in the attention.

I remember I wasn't jealous, even though I'm prone to jealousy.

I remember thinking he was better than me, and that was just the order of things.

I've worked at Julius Julius for more than fifty years. Nobody cares that I built the elevator. I've brought it up, at times, when I meet a younger colleague who seems interested in the agency's history. But nobody has ever thought to ask, *Hey, how did this elevator get here?*

A lot of people complain about it, though. They think the crank is old-fashioned and hard to turn, or they can't understand why it takes so long, or they're scared of the millipedes that crawl in through the grid of the cage.

I know it sounds strange, but that elevator is me. Me and a bunch of boys, many from my neighbourhood, many of whom have already lived and died. They're with me every time I get in, and they trail after me when I step out. They always recognize me, and they always take me back to who I was when I built it: vulnerable and unexceptional, but full of hope.

I don't remember much from our days in the cave. We weren't in there for very long. There were the white millipedes, and also bats. There were also these piles of bones. They were human bones, and they looked like they'd been there for a long time. We didn't know whose they were, or why they were there, but we were told they had to go. Our crew set to work shuttling them up, out, and onto a truck, where they would be taken to The Precinct, our neighbourhood, to be burned. I remember that some would shatter into dust when I touched them with my shovel.

Meanwhile, the art directors occupied themselves by wandering around the cave, kicking the lime walls, looking for the echo that meant a cavern. The idea was that we'd knock down a wall with a cavern behind it, and that would be the archives. A little crew, including the boy, followed the art directors around.

We found the wall with the cavern behind it on a Friday morning. I remember it being Friday morning because the boy and I had walked to work through a particularly golden sunrise, and he'd invited me to his father's birthday party the next day, Saturday. The family had not held a birthday party for anyone since the father had gotten back from the war, and the boy was excited.

When we got down into the cave, they had set us up in two workstations. I was on bone duty, which was usual for me.

The boy and the little crew he was part of were beckoned to the wall by one of the art directors and told to start in on it. About twelve boys were working on that wall, swinging their hammers in time.

They had rigged up some hanging oil lamps to give us some light. The art directors were wearing new hard hats with light bulbs attached to the brims, wandering around the scene, casting big light or big shadow wherever they looked.

The wall boys were singing a song to keep their swinging in time, and the rest of us bone boys joined in.

There was a loud noise, like a gun, a bang. We all turned when we heard it. The wall the boys had been hitting, which had looked solid just before, was now laced with cracks like an old teacup. They spread up to the ceiling of the cave. There was about one second where we were all just looking at that cracked wall, unsure of what was going to happen next.

We didn't have to wait long to find out. One little piece of the ceiling fell in the pond with a *plink*, then the rest of the ceiling fell, all at once, on top of the boys who had been hammering. If you'd blinked, you'd have thought they'd been whisked away and replaced by a pile of rocks.

The wall began to crumble, piling more rubble on top of them. I ran to try and do something and felt a tough haul on the back of my collar. One of the art directors was pulling me back toward the cave opening, where the rest of our crew was scrambling to get out.

We'll get them later, he said to me. *They'll be fine.*

I don't know what happened to my brain in that moment, but I believed him. We were shoved out the door, which they bolted shut.

Outside, the air was clear and the day was bright. We stood on the street outside the building, and it was as stable and permanent-looking as it had ever been. I could even see people working through the windows on the upper floors, though maybe that was my imagination, because I also seem to remember that they evacuated the building.

Spaghetti, Macaroni, and I walked home alone.

A group of men was allowed to go back into the cave to try to recover bodies. The boy's father was among them. It was thought that any impact might lead to further collapse, so the vinegar method was used to dissolve the lime rocks.

Heinz, expressing sympathy for the victims, donated 125 gallons of vinegar to the effort.

They found the bodies of everyone in the crew but the boy.

The National Lime and Chemical Company was founded in Richmond, Virginia, in 1890 by a group of miners. At the time, cities were growing, multiplying, and reaching up into the sky. That hasn't stopped.

Big, rich titans of industry began responding to the need for building materials by establishing mining operations that employed thousands of workers. Rather than working for one of these companies, miners in Virginia decided to start one themselves.

Stone gives a city a particular personality. St. Louis has a lot of red brick buildings, which give it a pragmatic, industrial feeling. Aberdeen in Scotland is largely built of granite, which is serious and moody.

Limestone is known for its bright, brilliant, and airy look. The pyramids of Giza are made of lime. So is most of Paris. I think a lime structure looks very ambitious and optimistic.

The National Lime and Chemical Company faced competition from companies that specialized in other building materials. They decided that the real money was in foundations, and crushed lime aggregate is one of the best—it's inexpensive, strong, and drains easily. So that was the objective with which the NL & CC came to us: they wanted to show builders that lime is the best choice for a foundation, and let the competitors fight it out over the facades.

It was my opinion that the National Lime and Chemical Company had another advantage. They weren't great and powerful men. They had been workers, just like the people who would be buying their products.

When I got the brief for the project, that was what moved me. I had been a worker; so had the boy. I wanted people to see us.

I was given the brief by one of the art directors who had been assigned to the elevator. I'm not ashamed to say that Spaghetti and I had been following him around, and when he asked me what I thought, it was a dream come true. We had almost finished the elevator, and I'd made my desire to be part of the agency clear. I had never been anywhere that felt both permanent and determined to be part of the future. I had always experienced my life as something that was happening just that day, and even that day wasn't guaranteed. That my feelings and ideas could echo into the future, attached to bags of coffee, bottles of honey liqueur, or foundations of limestone aggregate felt like a privilege.

This was the same art director who had installed the portrait in the elevator. Most people think it is a likeness of Julius Julius; it's actually the boy. That's the second most famous image of him, I guess. When we started work again after the accident, I was the only one who came back. I had no parents to stop me. This art director had drawn it and asked me for my opinion. I told him he'd made a picture of what almost was, and that seemed to move him. That's when he gave me the brief.

There's no pressure, he said, *just see if anything comes into your mind.*

I slept with that brief clutched in my hands. When I woke up, I thought of the photo of the boy standing on the rocks.

He had been a person who believed something good about the future. That's what the act of building is—an expression of hope for the future—because a building is a time traveller.

I went home and wrote the tagline "Strong foundations help us grow," imagining a parallel universe, one in which he had lived, and in which he had grown into everything he was supposed to be. He's standing on a pile of lime rubble, looking forward to the next day and all that it will bring, in a city full of buildings that he's made, seeing himself in every one of them.

If you hadn't known him, you could assume that it all happened. I'm sure most people do.

I

II

III *The Future Leader (Intern)*

I've been an intern for two years and three months. Except at Julius Julius, they don't call us interns; they call us Future Leaders. So, I've been a Future Leader for two years and three months. The joke my mom makes is that the future never comes.

The Future Leaders program is actually only supposed to be one year long. The idea is to get some work experience and then move on, which is why the program doesn't pay. The other people from my intern year all either got hired as permanent staff or got jobs at other agencies.

I thought for sure I would get hired, too. Midway through my first Future Leader year, my manager, who was really only in charge of me, went on some kind of stress leave and then just never came back. Then her manager asked if I could take on an entire account of hers, and I said, *Absolutely*, and to the best of my knowledge, I executed the tasks associated with that account perfectly and without complaint.

At the time, I felt lucky to have been handed an opportunity to impress my manager's manager. It was a big step up for me, and I was excited. I was put on Beefsteak Charlie's full-time, with the assignment of enticing a new generation of diners to get excited about old-fashioned steak houses. There was problem-solving, and I got to travel, and I supervised entire projects from start to finish.

When that first year was up, I was supposed to get a performance review. I did not, despite asking multiple times. When I see my old manager's manager in the halls, he acts hurried and annoyed and says something like *it's on our list*. But it must be pretty far down, because it's never happened.

I'm worried the reason I'm so far down on his list is because of what happened on the Fisherman Jack Tuna rebrand.

I was run over by a Jeep three months after I started advertising school. The guy almost drove right over my spine. I should be dead. The only reason I'm not: I had the expanded hardcover edition of *Hey Whipple, Squeeze This* in my backpack, and the tire went over that big thick book instead of me.

The author of *Hey Whipple* had come to our school that day for a Q & A, and I'd bought a copy and gotten it signed. It was a brand new book, so I hadn't even cracked the spine. How ironic, then, that it saved mine.

If I ever see the author again, that's what I'm going to say. I've heard he likes puns.

I had six broken ribs, a fractured sacrum, a fractured tibia, a broken fibula, a shattered kneecap, internal bleeding, a lot of bruising, road rash on one side of my face, and a shattered cheekbone on the other. I was in the hospital for months. I had to drop out of school and start again.

The driver felt terrible about running me over, especially after he learned I was the child of a single waitress. We settled out of court. The money was enough to pay for school and set me up for a while, at least until I find a job. A relief, because I don't have a salary.

By the way, the insight that drove the Fisherman Jack Tuna rebrand was my idea. The whole new creative platform that won all those awards? I thought of it. I know what's written on the award submissions, but it was me. Furthermore, despite all the posters on the walls about how this is the place where creativity meets purpose, that Fisherman Jack platform is the only meaningful work I've done in my entire time at JJ.

And even though the working process wasn't exactly fun and lighthearted, and despite how, at times, I had to go against the popular opinion of the team to get the best outcome, I think it's the best creative to come out of the agency in a decade.

Fisherman Jack Tuna has existed for more than seventy years. Cans of FJ sit in pantries all over the world. Fisherman Jack is stacked on shelves in food banks and bomb shelters. I wouldn't be surprised to learn they took that tuna to space.

Fisherman Jack was a real fisherman. He's not some marketing executive's creation, like Betty Crocker. Fisherman Jack lived and died on the sea. He came to America with just one boat and made his fortune in Monterey, California, at the turn of the century.

Initially, he had intended to get into the sardine business. That was the predominant canned fish on the market those days. Sardines were durable, portable, and salty. But they had also been overfished, and the market was saturated with sardine brands.

So, Jack thought to himself, *what else can I put in a can?*

Tuna fish was known to be delicious, but the fish were extremely hard to catch. Tuna are fast swimmers and they prefer deep waters.

In a moment of quiet contemplation, Jack observed that tuna ate the little guppies that swam close to the surface of the water.

Jack and his crew invented a new method of fishing. First, they would catch hundreds of those surface-swimming guppies. They would wait for daybreak, when the sun glittered on the water, then scatter the guppies overboard, casting fishing hooks at the same time. The hungry tuna would race to the surface, dazzled by the abundance of guppies, and bite frantically, indiscriminately—including at the hooks. Jack and his crew would reel them in by the dozens. A proprietary tactic was born. Jack became the tuna king of Monterey.

I adore the can's design, which has only changed once in seventy years. The label depicts Fisherman Jack wearing a wool cap with a brim. His expression is hopeful, peaceful, and a little melancholic. Behind him is the Pacific Ocean. In the distance, we see his boat. The boat is flying the Monterey county flag—which bears six tunas and three waves, representing the bounty of the waters—implying Jack's role in the town's economic prosperity.

Some people have objected to the absence of sardines on the flag of Monterey. They were the most populous and abundant fish in the region for so long, and the foundational catch for the majority of the area's fishermen. Populations moved to the area and supported themselves on sardines for decades. So why wouldn't there be at least one sardine on the region's flag?

A little-known fact: the flag of Monterey didn't exist before Fisherman Jack's iconic can design. The can predates the flag by eighteen years. The county flag took its design from the can.

In the early days of my work on this rebrand, I thought we should do some research on the can's artist. No one else on the team seemed to believe the artist was an important part of the brand story. But this artist's hand had unknowingly designed the flag of Monterey and had influenced people's impressions of FJ for decades, so I gave myself the job of learning about him.

I had to sneak into the archives of Bekerman Ennis Damgaard Gudrunas, which was FJ's previous agency. We had only recently been awarded the business following a pitch. We were asked to start the rebrand straight away, but the people at BEDG were slow to hand over the files. So I went undercover.

I had never been inside another ad agency. Julius Julius is the only place I've ever worked.

I was worried I'd get caught, but I shouldn't have been. BEDG isn't as big as Julius Julius, but it's bustling. I think five hundred people must work there, and every single one of them looks beautiful enough to be on TV.

BEDG's office is modern, angular, and full of light. It's also extremely easy to navigate. They've painted big yellow arrows on the floor to direct you anywhere you need to go. I had no trouble finding the archives, which are in a spacious and sunny library full of overstuffed pink sofas. No one asked to see my ID. I don't think anyone even looked at me. I just strolled in, pulled the Fisherman Jack file, sat on a sofa, and read. It was heaven.

The artist who designed the can we all know and love today? None other than Fisherman Jack's son, Jack Jr.

I know, I was shocked, too.

Employees of Julius Julius have access to a discounted membership at SweatBlitz Gyms. Few take advantage of the deal, but I do. I go to the location across the street, which you can access via one of the cave tunnels, so you don't even have to go outside.

It's not a luxury place, but it's got all the basic amenities. I like that I don't feel pressure to show off in expensive workout gear. I see a guy from the mailroom on the treadmill, sometimes. He jogs in his corduroys.

After my accident, I took up swimming. I used to run, but when my feet pound on the ground, I can feel where my bones were broken. When I'm swimming, I don't even feel like I have a body. SweatBlitz has a huge pool, and it's almost always completely empty.

I have only ever seen one other person at the pool, and even then, I'm not actually sure I saw them. I was alone, as usual, doing laps. I felt someone tap me on the heel to pass me, and then I felt them pass me, but when I got to the end of the lane, there was no one there.

The agency is basically overflowing with ghosts, and it wouldn't surprise me if some of them had started haunting the gym, just for a change of scenery.

Jack Jr. was born in Monterey and spent his childhood on his father's fishing boat. By the time Jr. was six, the family business was successful.

Other fathers might have expected their sons to take over the boat, but Fisherman Jack recognized that his was drawn to softer pursuits and encouraged his early love of painting. When it came time to redesign the Fisherman Jack can, father awarded son the job.

It turned out to be a smart move on Jack's part, because his son's portrait and design made him a global icon, one of the richest men in the world, and a legend whose face has been trusted for decades.

I support this agency. It was me who cared for Cannellini, the oldest of the dogs, when she got sick. I'm the one who took her for her very slow walks. I'm the one who crushed omega-3 supplements into her food to help reduce the inflammation in her joints and paws from spending her whole life walking up and down the agency stairs. I'm the one who took her to the vet and then to my home after because she was scared. I'm the one who lets her sleep in my bed because the agency floors are too hard for her old bones.

I know what it's like to be fragile, pitiful, a burden. People won't tell you *hey, I pity you, you're burdening me*, but you know when you're walking down the sidewalk at your best pace and other pedestrians pass you with a huff and what they think is a subtle shake of the head.

Everybody in this agency goes gooey for the puppies. The old dogs get ignored. But the old dogs are the ones who have guarded this place, barked at the ghosts, had their tails pulled and their collars stolen by drunken clients at the holiday parties. And they don't even get to retire. They just live out their days in a forest of ankles, no hands reaching down to scratch their ears.

I know I'm not everyone's cup of tea. I've never been a popular person. Even before my accident, I would have described myself as a cautious type A. But I take my work seriously. I try to get things right. I believe I owe it to myself and everyone else here to do my best.

So no, I don't make a lot of jokes or laugh at many jokes. The other Future Leaders from my year still go to the Blue Toot Pub every Thursday. They stopped inviting me months ago. I'm awkward, and I'm not outgoing or witty, which is the social currency at this place. But I always believed that my colleagues appreciate my passion for our work and this agency. I don't know how they all seem so casual and happy. This kind of workplace isn't designed to nurture happiness. That's not a bad thing. The entire structure of this place and the work we do here is about climbing and striving and competing. Personally, I think that if you're content, you're doing it wrong.

I understand now that advertising is a celebrity system. The industry loves its little star geniuses. And despite what I thought, you don't get to be a little star genius by putting in the hours or taking on the hard jobs. No. To be a star you actually do the opposite. You stay out of the muck. You cultivate your charisma. You make everyone laugh.

Take, for instance, my old manager's manager, who put me on Fisherman Jack. He is charming. He is tall. Every single person on his team loves him. And yet I would challenge any of them to name a single piece of work he has contributed to this project.

I'm talking about work that he's done that came from his own head. He's passed off many of my ideas as his own.

He has never made a workback schedule or written a contact report or even said anything in a client call that somebody else didn't say first. It simply doesn't matter; he just keeps getting promotions.

His success makes me doubt my entire value system. Are any of the things I like about myself actually worth liking? Are the ethics and habits I spend so much time cultivating going to get me anywhere?

When I first became his direct report, after my original manager left on stress leave, I had a crush on him. That is humiliating for me to admit, now.

Back then, we spent a lot of time together on Beefsteak Charlie's. I was happy to do whatever he asked of me, especially because it meant I got to be with him.

We travelled together.

We would be flown out to locations all over the prairies: Minnetonka, Wichita, Saskatoon. These trips might not sound romantic to most people, but I lost myself in those great expanses of land. The quiet of the deep snow, the bigness of the sky, even the consistency of the Beefsteak Charlie's chain was meaningful to me. Every restaurant was the same, and every one of them was ours.

I remember one particular dinner well. We had eaten from the same menu so many times that he took a guess and ordered for me. The food he'd chosen wasn't what I wanted, but I went with it because I was thrilled he'd paid attention to what I liked.

We talked until we were the last table and the restaurant was closing. He told me all about his childhood, his family, and a girl he'd wanted in his first year of university who hadn't wanted him back. I said, *I'm sure she wanted you a little bit, everybody does.* In response, he pretended to get flustered. I was the flustered one; it's out of character for me to say flirtatious things.

I remember how the pillar candle on the table burned down to a little wax disc. I tried to steal it at the end of the night as a souvenir, but it was really stuck to the candle holder and I couldn't fit the whole thing in my purse.

He used to say he loved me. I couldn't tell if it was as a friend or more. It didn't matter. The way he said it, full eye contact, very sincere, made my heart flutter.

I know, I'm stupid.

This is how a charming person charms: they make you feel like you're important to them. But at the same time, they're making everyone else feel the same amount of important. So when the charming person walks into a room, people light up. Because that's what you do when someone makes you feel special. And, of course, you don't know that you're just part of everyone.

The world is careless. Not malevolent, just careless. People who bump into you on the street don't mean harm, even though they cause it.

When you think you have found a person who cares about you, your world changes. And when it fades away, you realize that the care was as random as the carelessness.

Julius Julius   277

Julius Julius is always hiring. There's never a slump. That's because we take a lot of sediment work. Most of us in advertising are shovelling sediment.

This agency takes every flyer campaign, every coupon writing assignment, every pamphlet creation initiative. We have clients like the American Parking Lot Federation and MWW Manufacturing, which makes tubular gas burners for restaurants in long-term care facilities. There are departments dedicated to writing the letters that describe all the features of those tubular gas burners so they are tailored to a person who runs a kitchen at a nursing home. I know, I started in that department.

You can do a little bit of this kind of work, but when you do too much, you drift to the bottom.

To do the exciting, culturally significant work, you have to seem like the kind of person who could get the attention of everyone in the world, because that's what good ads do.

For the rest of us, there's sediment.

A hiring manager doesn't need to find you charming or compelling to believe you could effectively work in a department of people who describe oven parts.

The partners would never assign my old manager's manager to sediment work. They couldn't imagine him even knowing what oven tubes are. They see themselves in him, and they don't know.

When people ask me, I tell them I chose to do my internship at Julius Julius because it seemed stable. You can't argue with a place that's been continuously operating for almost 2,000 years. *They're doing something right, business-wise*, I say. But the truth is, no one else wanted me. I reached out to dozens of other agencies, tried to have coffee with so many different recruiters. No one took me up on my invitation.

We write a brief at the beginning of each new project. This involves filling out a template. It's supposed to describe the client's business problem in a way that will inspire a creative team to make work that's engaging and impactful. Our template is called the PIIP, which stands for Priority, Issue, Insight, Proposition. You write a line under each heading, and that's your brief.

The PIIP Brief

Priority:
The business goal as it relates to the target audience.

Issue:
What's the problem we need to solve to get the audience to change their perceptions?

Insight:
A deep understanding articulated as a truth that unlocks an evolution of our target audience's relationship to the brand.

Proposition:
How we activate the insight to shift perceptions or behaviours.

The FJ clients were a cluster of sad-sack businessmen with sweaters under their blazers. Apparently, Jack's granddaughter still sits on the board. I've seen a photo of her dressed in pink silk perched on the corner of a desk that looks out over the sea. She didn't come to our meeting.

The clients told us that sales had been declining for more than a decade. Brand perceptions were negative, and FJ was perceived as a processed corporate food. Recent years had seen a pivot to salmon in the category because—and this is the worst part—tuna fishing was seen as bad for the environment. People were concerned about the ocean floor; people were worried about dolphins.

There was conversation on the team about how we should write the PIIP brief to change people's perceptions. Could we redesign the label to include a healthy, smiling dolphin? Could we create a pamphlet that told the real-life story of Fisherman Jack? Could we run an anti-salmon campaign?

It was my strong opinion that the opportunity on Fisherman Jack was much bigger than an anti-salmon campaign. Generations have stirred this tuna into casseroles. Generations have spread a mix of this tuna, some mayonnaise, and some relish between two pieces of whole wheat bread. I ate this tuna every day when I was in grade school. It means a lot to me.

Much of my childhood is wrapped up in memories of Fisherman Jack. Stacks of cans in the pantry. Jack's wise face on the label. The smell of it.

My mother sent me to school with a tuna salad sandwich every day. My school didn't provide a fridge for students to store their lunches in, so they sat in a hot closet at the back of the room. By the time noon came, my sandwich was fragrant, and the other kids would complain. Most days, the teacher would send me outside to eat by myself because otherwise, she said, my food would stink up the room.

I didn't mind going outside. I sat under a big tree with my back to the classroom window, away from the chaos and screaming kids whipping bologna and Fruit Roll-Ups at each other. Lunch hour in elementary school is hell.

I was an unlikeable child. All of my clothes were brightly coloured atrocities from the discount department store, stained and pill-balled. I had a lot of shirts with a big word and an exclamation point printed across them, like "Fun!" or "Tokyo!" My hair was unbrushed. I hated to be in bright lighting or large groups of people. I wasn't cute. I didn't like to talk.

I sometimes imagine myself as another child in my cohort with lots of friends and a kitchen full of non-tuna fish food. I imagine myself as that other child seeing me. I can understand the disgust.

I am different now. I am organized, and I do things to take care of myself. Not just my physical self, although that is a big part of the change. I learned to invest in basic, high-quality staples that never look out of place. Tailored shirts, nude heels, pencil skirts.

There is a junior project manager on our team who is very ambitious, but completely unimaginative. Everything she suggests is something that's already been done, so everyone thinks she's rational.

She asked to lead the writing of the PIIP brief. My old manager's manager is unthreatened by her, so he said yes. Her insight was tedious and functional, all about how Fisherman Jack was a family business that makes seafood affordable.

Of course, he loved her brief, because he loves when things are easy.

I'm sorry, but a seventy-year-old tuna brand caught up in the midst of a critical conversation about the evils of processed foods and ocean conservation is not actually an easy problem to solve. For people to love Fisherman Jack again, they need to feel an emotional shift. Spouting facts at consumers won't get them to change their behaviour.

In the early days of the Fisherman Jack project, I was depressed. I didn't know that at the time. I often have difficulty naming my feelings.

I'm routine-driven. I wake up at 7 a.m. I go for a walk outside.
I eat a bowl of Vector High Protein Cereal with skim milk and
drink a cup of black coffee.

I take the streetcar to work; travel time is forty-five minutes.
I get a second cup of black coffee in the work kitchen, and in
that cup goes a half packet of Sweet'N Low. I put the other half
in my purse.

I sit down at my desk, read memos, and return calls. I do not
get up from my desk until lunch. For lunch, I get an egg salad
or tuna fish sandwich from the café downstairs.

I try to schedule all my meetings in the afternoon, that's my
least favourite part of the day.

I go swimming in the SweatBlitz pool at 5:15 p.m., that's my
most favourite part of the day.

I go back to the agency to dry my hair and maybe walk
Cannellini around the block, if she's feeling energetic. I work
until 8 p.m., undisturbed by the commotion of other people.

I take the streetcar home, where I read or listen to CDs and
cook dinner.

Once a month, I go on a date. They are generally flops, but I
know that this is the time in my life when I should be trying
to find love.

Sometime after the junior project manager presented her brief, new thoughts began to find their way into my routine. I'd be in the agency kitchen and think, *What if I pour this hot coffee down the collar of my blouse and it leaves a river of blisters and burned skin?* I'd be in the middle of a conference call and ask myself, *What if I smash my phone into tiny pieces and then eat the pieces? Will that kill me? What if I did it very slowly, over the course of days?*

These kinds of thoughts are not normal for me. They made me realize that in a previous iteration of myself, I rarely had thoughts; I mostly just had responses. What were these new thoughts a response to?

You know how we are 80% water? I've heard that so often I thought it must be a lie, but it's true. I looked it up.

One day, while I was swimming, I tried to let myself sink to the bottom of the pool. I kept floating back to the surface. Every time I'd try to sink, the water would lift me up.

I had this thought: *The water supports me.* And then I thought to myself, *Because I am the water.*

I got out of the pool, but I didn't dry off. I put my clothes on over my wet bathing suit. I walked back through the tunnel, feeling the cool underground air chill the wet fabric against my skin.

I sat at my desk and studied the Fisherman Jack label. He is in the foreground, looking at whoever is holding the can. His eyes, however, beckon the viewer to look past him, to the fishing boat. Because the boat is where Fisherman Jack really is. It's where his spirit is free and his purpose is realized. Some men name their boats after their wives. Fisherman Jack's boat has no name. Just a flag that's an ode to the waters, his work, and the fish in the can.

Nothing and no one else matter. His son must have been so lonely.

I never break protocol. But I could not let the junior project manager tank an incredible opportunity for our team and agency with some dry-as-dust value-focused brief for Fisherman Jack.

I wrote my own brief, and I presented it to the partners in a secret meeting that I booked without the rest of the team's knowledge.

The PIIP Brief:
Fisherman Jack Tuna Rebrand

Priority:
Re-establish Fisherman Jack as a nutrition leader for our target: health-conscious enviro-crusaders aged 25–65.

Issue:
Our target believes tuna fishing practices are detrimental to the ocean's ecosystem and has been pivoting to salmon.

Insight:
Our relationship to the sea is ancient and essential. Water is part of us, and water is always beckoning us back. Eating tuna is a way to connect to the water and, therefore, to our deepest, most fundamental selves.

Proposition:
Get our target to reimagine the act of eating Fisherman Jack Tuna as a means to forge a connection to the seas rather than as an act of destroying them.

I read the brief aloud in the room for the partners. They all got quiet.

That's going to win a lot of awards, one of them said. The others nodded.

That's going to boost sales, another said.

And they all nodded.

You're in the Future Leaders program? one of them asked.

Yes, for almost two years now, I said.

We're going to keep our eye on you, said another of the partners. And the rest of them nodded.

When my manager's manager heard what I'd done, he was angry. I don't know that because he told me; I know that because he stopped speaking to me. He had booked his own meeting with the partners to take them through the brief the junior project manager had written. The partners were confused.

Let's stick to the original brief, they said, gesturing to me.

Of course, he said. And that settled the matter.

I presented my brief to the creative team, they got to work, and my manager's manager stopped inviting me to meetings.

I could have been a little star genius, too. Did anybody ever think of that? If someone had spent the time and coached me, I could have developed my soft skills. That would have made me unstoppable.

I want to say something like *I am so sorry for caring*, but that's not even it. I am somehow always too much. Even in this situation, when I know I'm acting in everyone's best interests. Why can't he see that?

There are still sardine fishing operations in Monterey. They're not as robust as they once were, but they exist. In the early days of our rebrand, I got myself a subscription to *Coastal Fishing* magazine. In the August issue, sort of shoved toward the back, was an article about a cluster of sardine fisheries and canneries on the rocky shores near the southern edge of town. One of them, Lee's Best Sardines, has been operating continuously since the 1870s. It's still a family-owned business, and the family is still involved in the day-to-day.

The can is a rectangular flat pack with a pull tab. On the top is a pen and ink illustration of a silvery sardine, his eyes bright and urgent.

The Lee family is optimistic about the future of sardines in Monterey. While they have been alone in their category for decades, recent years have seen an increase in the sardine population. New fisheries have been established. An emergent consumer trend for generationally nostalgic foods means that sardines are making their way toward a humble culinary stardom.

For the first few days after I shared my brief, I thought my calendar had gone quiet because the team needed to absorb the profundity of what I'd written. But when eight days had passed and I hadn't been invited to a creative check-in or review, I knew something was wrong.

I had long ago reserved the Aquarium meeting room for our project, because the name was cute and relevant. The room was called the Aquarium because it had four glass walls.

On the eighth day of silence, I walked by and saw, through the glass walls, the entire team meeting without me. A full creative review, with art on boards and scripts and presenters, was taking place. The junior project manager was taking notes. My manager's manager was leaning forward, gesturing with his hands.

Everyone in the room turned their heads slowly, looked at me standing outside the glass, and wordlessly agreed to ignore me, as though I was a ghost. They just went back to work on the brief that I had written.

It wasn't just the meetings; the entire team stopped speaking to me. They would avoid me in the halls; they'd see me coming and pretend to shuffle papers.

They stopped meeting in the Aquarium and took to gathering in more and more obscure parts of the agency. I saw them doing what looked like consumer journey mapping under the big conference table in the King Koffee boardroom.

Under the table? Really? You think I'm going to crawl under the stupid table and try to take part in your little exercise? I can tell when I'm not wanted.

Of course my heart broke when I saw the creative. The work that came from the brief I wrote was moving and disruptive.

The hero was a TV spot in which we see Fisherman Jack in his iconic boat. He's frustrated because there haven't been any bites in a long time. He peers over the boat's edge to the deepest waters, and there he sees the glimmer of silvery scales. He's pulled overboard, and the fish carries him down to the ocean floor, where he joins a party of dancing, singing tuna. They bring him to a throne made of Fisherman Jack Tuna cans and crown him king. There's a super at the end that reads "We've always been loved by the sea."

There was also a series of billboards bearing lines like "80% water? You've always been loved by the sea" and "Ancestors were fish? You've always been loved by the sea."

The team also commissioned a 100-foot-high statue of Fisherman Jack, which they placed just off the shore of the beach at Monterey. The statue was made entirely of mirrors, intimating that Jack was the sea, and the sea was Jack. It looked extraordinary, but it had to be taken down because seabirds kept starting fights with their reflections.

You have to be very careful about with whom you share the deep, personal details of yourself. Not everyone deserves them. I've learned the hard way.

I imagine Jack Jr. preparing to paint his father. They're in a studio filled with that particular grey-gold North Coast California light. Jr. has asked Sr. to wear what he wears at sea, an ensemble that's both familiar to him and symbolic of his father's distance from him. When Jack Sr. sits, the smell of salt water, of fish, of young crew members he may also call "son" comes in with him.

Jr. says to Sr., *Now look at me*, but Jack Sr. looks past his son to the window, where his boat dances on the water.

I imagine after Jr. gets his father's likeness, he turns his seat toward that window, too, so that he can see his father's boat out on the horizon. He paints every plank, every rivet, every rope. Despite this meticulous effort, he thinks to himself, *There's something missing, still.*

His father's essence cannot be captured in a representation of his face. His father's essence cannot even be captured in an image of the boat that he loves. At the core of his father is the drive to succeed, to see below the surface of the waters to a new conquest, to those thrashing schools of tuna, bountiful for the taking if one can only figure out how.

On a whim, Jack Jr. paints a flag that does not exist. That flag is a rebrand of its own, making a place that was known for sardines known instead for the story of his father's tuna conquest. As though there had been no stories before his family's story.

That flag is woven and flown on every boat and at the gate of the cannery. Then it's flown outside other canneries, then on the streets and in the town square during homecoming, then on the big flagpole on the rocky shores at the southern end of town, where Lee's Best Sardines still operates.

Lee's Best Sardines: surviving for decades in the shadow of Fisherman Jack's bulging enterprise. A small family sardinerie continuing operations because this is what they've always done and what's the point of quitting, anyway? They're not going to learn a new business. They knew through all those years that if the time to prosper wasn't now, it would one day come. They had prospered in the past, hadn't they? It's not as though people are going to quit eating. Someday mouths will water for the briny and oily again.

After the initial rush of success on the campaign, I made the mistake of trying to establish some peace between my manager's manager and me. It did not go well. My emotions took over.

I had been told to distribute a memo alerting the entire agency to the fact that *You've Always Been Loved by the Sea* swept the awards season with multiple golds and best in shows. I was happy to read it, despite the fact that he was given full and almost solo credit.

This wasn't what I planned, but I walked up to his desk holding a stack of those memos and I burst into tears. I wept. And he just sat there and watched me. He didn't offer a Kleenex or reach out a hand to comfort me. And during the long walk back to my own desk, everyone noticed me, but no one acknowledged me. That happens when you're on the outs at work. Your colleagues get afraid that your undesirability is contagious.

I feel so angry at myself when I wake up from dreaming about my manager's manager. It happens pretty often, no matter how many times I tell myself not to dream about him. They are not necessarily romantic dreams, although I still feel rejected in them.

In the most recent one, I was standing outside the glass boardroom. He was sitting inside, looking at some work in a folder. That tedious junior project manager appeared beside me and said, *How could you betray him? He's done so much for you.* Of course, my voice stops working, as it so often does in dreams, I try to say, *I didn't mean to, I love him.* But I can't get the words out. She then walks into the room, and he greets her warmly and tilts his folder so she can see what's inside.

I woke up with my heart absolutely slamming against my chest in my apartment full of affordable chipboard starter furniture.

Cannellini, who had been sleeping beside me after a visit to the vet, curled her little bean of a body into the hollow space in mine.

Bring your whole self to work. Isn't that one of the platitudes on the mural behind reception? I don't think they mean that.

I was contacted by a recruiter a few weeks ago about an opportunity to be the marketing manager at Lee's Best Sardines. I couldn't believe it. Apparently they had seen the Fisherman Jack campaign, and the call had been directed my way. They weren't looking for a creative team or an inspiring leader; they needed someone to do, as it was put to me, the dirty work of getting the brand back on track. They needed a budget in place, and to establish a direct mail program, and to build relationships with local grocery stores. It's not the most glamorous job, but I will, once again, have the opportunity to contribute to a brand with an incredible legacy.

I've accepted the offer, which means I'll be moving to Monterey. I put in a request to officially adopt Cannellini, and I was granted permission. Apparently no one in the history of the agency has ever before been successful in their attempt to adopt one of the dogs. She's almost fourteen years old, though, so they made an exception. One of the other dogs just had a litter of puppies so everyone is distracted, and they figure she's only got another year. Cannellini and I are going to spend it together on the beach, where she'll get salt water in her fur and the sand will be soft under her old paws.

Acknowledgements

I cannot believe my good luck, to have been surrounded by so many people who cared for me during the writing and selling and preparing of this book.

Thank you to my beloved husband Scott and his deep patience and support. I'm so grateful to have written this book in our apartment while he was in the other room.

Thank you to Mom, Dad, Terry, Slater, and especially Niccola, for talking to me about construction and elevator installation. Thank you Bruce Barber, me doing any of this was your idea.

Thank you to my friends who read the book and talked it into something real over dinners and walks. I took your advice, Serah-Marie McMahon, Lauren Bride, Nika Mistruzzi, Emily Keeler, Alex Molotkow, Vanessa Magic, Celina Bussière, Michal Fetsum, Jess Salgueiro, Stephanie Damgaard, Simon Ennis, Gwyneth Tossel, Jill Holmberg, Julia Lederer, Sara Spears, Gustavo Cerquera Benjumea, Chandler Levack, Cara Gee and especially you, angel Naomi Skwarna.

Thank you to all the people I have loved in advertising. Amanda Buchanan, most of all. You believed in me, and I would have never had the opportunities and experiences I did if it hadn't

320   *Acknowledgements*

been for you. I am so grateful to you for seeing me differently than I saw myself. Thank you to Randy Byers, who told me about sappers.

Thank you to Dougie the Dog, the all-time most perfect agency dog, and whose gentle behaviours and long, silky ears were the inspiration for the dogs in this book.

Thank you to Rebecca Rooney, Sarah Stinnissen, and Mariana Diez de Bonilla.

Thank you to Jaime Nikolaou and Sarah Campbell for being the only possible team I could ever have had for headshots.

Thank you Matthew Flute for the perfect cover design: an elegant, mysterious dog butt that I was so excited to share. Thank you to Lorissa Sengara and Crissy Boylan for your meticulous care and edits. Thank you to Tonia Addison, Sarah Howland, Hannah Karpinski, Kimberlee Kemp, Kim Kandravy, Adeeba Noor, Taylor Rice, Brayden Ross, Rebecca Rocillo and Sean Tai.

Thank you to my editor at Strange Light, Haley Cullingham, who believed in this book as soon as it crossed her desk and has been a champion and protector of its pages ever since. It is my extreme good fortune to have stumbled into your world. Thank you to my wonderful agent Cody Caetano, who discussed every single word with me and who kindly, determinedly ensured that this book would be a book even during a time when it threatened to stay a word doc. You have been a steady source of assurance and optimism. Thank you to Stephanie Sinclair, who, as we've moved through time together, has gently pushed boulders away from seemingly sealed entrances to let the light in. You have been there the whole time, thank god.